DIRTY WOLF

AN ALPHA WOLVES WANT CURVES NOVEL

AIDY AWARD

Publisher's Note: This is a work of fiction. Names, characters, places, and incidents are a product of the author's imagination. Locales and public names are sometimes used for atmospheric purposes. Any resemblance to actual people, living or dead, or to businesses, companies, events, institutions, or locales is completely coincidental.

Dirty Wolf/ Aidy Award. -- 1st ed.

Cover by Jacqueline Sweet

For my best writer buddies Ann and Hopey

Fall like a thunderbolt.

—Sun Tzu

WOLVES, DRINKS, AND OTHER DELICIOUS THINGS

*A*hh. Finally she could breathe. The cool night air brought the heat in her cheeks and her temper down to a manageable level. Gal seriously knew better than to walk through the Reserve at night, but here she was. The posted rules stated that the area closed at dusk, and trespassers would face severe consequences. Lately that kind of threat meant less and less to her. After the blowout she'd had with her dad tonight, she was feeling an extra special kind of rebelliousness and consequences could go blow themselves.

So, yeah. She'd snuck out of her room like some teenager, and cut through the Reserve even though it was nine o'clock at night and dusk had long since come and gone. But come on, seriously. What twenty-three year old woman with an advanced degree wasn't allowed out at night to hang with her friends?

Her. That's who.

She found herself stomping, but it wouldn't do to trample some poor little caterpillar or crush some flowers because of her foul mood. It wasn't their fault. It was hers for not realizing what moving in with her parents would be like. She was saving every nickel and dime that didn't go toward paying her school loan. She'd sold her car to save on gas and insurance since she lived within walking distance to the library. Tonight was the first time since she'd gotten back to Rogue that she'd even gone out. It wasn't like she wasn't trying.

Trying too hard according to her dad, who'd told her more than once tonight she was making him bald. What really irked her was that her mother had simply sat there on the couch, knitting of all things, and hadn't said a word as her father had berated her lifestyle. Choosing to get a masters degree in Library Science and not being married were not bad choices. Ugh.

Unless your father would rather have you still a virgin, married to a nice Persian boy, and staying at home doing the dishes. No way, *pedar*.

A rustling behind her in the underbrush had her speeding up. If she made as much noise as possible, maybe that would scare away any animals following her. Eek, she hoped it was an animal. As far as she knew, Rogue, New York had never had a serial killer. Double eek. Maybe that meant they were due for one.

The leaves on the trees shivered in the wind and the shadows in the underbrush seemed much darker than they should. She was such a freaking dumb bunny. She should have just called an Uber to take her to the old town district. It just felt so deliciously naughty to do a little law breaking in what had felt like a benign way at the time.

Now here she was in the middle of the dark forest of the Reserve and pretty sure someone or something was following her. Gal whipped out her phone and dialed Zara's number. "Come on, come on. Pick up."

She really wished that she hadn't listened to those teenagers at the library last week who insisted these woods were filled with wolves. No, not just wolves, werewolves. She'd laughed along with the kids and helped them find a werewolf anime series to read. Might as well take advantage of their fascination with the supernatural to get them to read.

If they were right and she got bit by some creepy ass animal and turned into a shape shifter, she was going to.... to.... kill someone. Gal laughed at her own ridiculousness and dialed the phone again. Zara picked up and the sounds of a busy bar burst through the phone.

"Hey, where are you?" Her friend shouted into the phone.

"On my way. I had a big fight with my dad, but I'll be there soon. I could seriously use a drink." And to have her head examined. And a drink.

Something swished across the path behind her and her conversation went on autopilot while her brain compiled a to-do list for escape and evading. She said the required yeses, nos, and kept her voice cheery, but she also hurried a little bit faster. The instructor at the all women's martial arts school she'd taken classes at in Ann Arbor would be really disappointed if her star student was murdered because she's made a really bad decision to go out walking alone after dark.

In the woods.

Where werewolves lived.

Don't be silly. Gal could still use the skills she'd learned in class about spatial awareness and threat assessment to get out of the Reserve safely. The first thing was to make sure her friends knew exactly where she was. She spoke so loudly, the

whole city would know her position. Take that weird, creepy
stalker.

"Yeah, ha ha. I'm almost to the parking lot at the edge of
the Reserve." She could see the lights of the businesses in the
old town district and the road up ahead. She was going to
make it and without spotting any monsters of any kind.

That's when she caught sight of the wolf.

She barely glimpsed him out of the corner of her eye. A
flash of silver against the brown and green of the forest.

She waited for her heart to stop, for the scream from the
innermost depths of her soul, or to simply faint right there on
the little dirt path.

None of those things happened.

A sense of calm, like she'd been hit in the face with a whole
lavender bush, washed through her. She had zero doubts that
the animal was there to protect her, not harm her. What a
strange thing to think, but she knew it was true.

Clearly she was hallucinating and needed that drink more
than she thought she did. Moving back home, starting a new
job, and saying goodbye to her care-free and independent
college life had taken more of a toll on her psyche than she
had previously thought. Time to de-stress with a good old
girls night out.

In a few more feet she was in the parking lot and jogging
across the street. Her favorite little bar, the Sleepy Folk, an old
speakeasy from the days of prohibition was just another block
up the street. She pushed into the little pie shop at the front
and headed straight for the back stairs that led to the bar
below. Although, later she was totally having a fried apple pie.
Mmm. Two in the morning, slightly tipsy, bar food was the
best.

She should know, her ass showed just how much she liked tasty beverages and tasty treats. Not that she'd been a skinny-mini to start out with, but she'd put on the freshman fifteen and more. Her college friends had gotten her hooked on sweet shots and she'd never looked back.

The bar was packed but Zara and Heli had a coveted table and spotted her right away. Zara waved and Gal pushed through the Friday night crowd to get to them. They were the best of friends and had her chocolate martini waiting. She'd taarof with them later to decide who paid. "Hi, you guys. I missed you both so much."

They all went in for a round of hugs. Heli first, then Zara who held on for longer than the regular old friend reunion squeeze. Seems they all needed a girls night out. Fruity flavored alcohol was a great cure all. When Zara released her, Gal raised her glass and they clinked glasses. "To many more girls nights out."

"I'll drink to that," Heli said and sipped her pink drink. Zara's beverage looked quite a bit stronger. Something amber on ice. Whiskey. Yikes. Hanging out with her friends when they weren't drinking moved up on the priority list. She'd do her best to pull whatever was wrong out of Zara later.

Gal squeezed Zara's hand and made a silent promise to be there for her. "Okay. I want all the town gossip from you two. Six years is far too long to be gone. Give me the low down on who is sleeping with whom and who else is mad about it. The preschoolers at story time don't know squat. Totally unreliable for gossip, those kids are."

Heli exhaled and smiled, a thank you in her eyes. "Well. Remember Cynthia, third in line for the mean girl title my year?"

"The one who bleached her hoo-ha so her carpet would match her curtains?" They all knew, because every horny jock on the football, basketball, baseball, and even the soccer team knew. High school boys were worse gossips than any of them ever were.

"Yeah." Heli rubbed her hands together and her eyes flashed with the kind of mischief Gal loved her for. "She married Mark Grubler."

"No." Gal gasped in fun. "But his family is uber religious. He used to go to church before school every morning."

Heli took another sip of her drink and popped a piece of fruit in her mouth, chewing and making them wait. "I know, Cyn is a devout Sunday school teacher now and the perfect little homemaker. She's the president of the PTA."

"How is that even possible? You have to have a child enrolled.... oh. What? They were doing it in high school?"

Zara laughed and finally joined in the conversation. "Yep. Little Noah is six and started first grade this year. He's some sort of math prodigy or something. Can you even imagine?"

They giggled and laughed and gossiped until Gal's cheeks hurt. Man, she needed this. She absolutely needed to make more time to hang out with her friends and rekindle all the good times they had together. Who would have thought three girls who'd bonded over the horrors of the aerobics unit in their mandatory high school PE class would be such good friends after six years apart?

"Speaking of old gossip. Look who just walked in." Heli gave the tiniest of motions with her head behind Gal. "Wait. Don't just turn around and stare. Be cool about it."

Cool? Right. Gal picked up her glass, downed the rest so it

was empty and turned toward the bar like she was going to get another one.

Standing where she expected to see the bartender was the boy, uh- huge, hot, man...., had he gained a lot of muscle..., man she'd had a crush on since about the third grade. He caught her looking and his eyelids lowered to half-hooded and he grinned.

Every butterfly in the northern hemisphere flew straight into her stomach and a good fifty percent of those migrated south. Gal spun around and widened her eyes at Heli. "You could have told me it was Max. Cripes. He isn't coming over here, is he?"

Heli nodded. "He sure is."

"Ack. Do I have anything in my teeth? Did I spill down the front of my shirt. Dirt on my head, I always do that."

The words poured out of Heli's mouth, hurrying to answer. "You look great. His mouth is probably already watering. Here he comes."

"Ladies." A hand landed on the back of her chair and she could practically feel the heat coming off his extreme hotness. "Can I get you another round?"

"Hi Max. That's nice of you." Heli grinned up at Max. Gal didn't have the guts to do the same.

"Heli, Zara." Max gave Zara a bit of a nod and a conspiratorial grin. The Troikas' parents had never approved of Max's older brother Niko and Zara seeing each other. Max and Kosta didn't agree with their parents. One time they even pretended to have a broken down car in the next town over to get their mom and dad out of the house so Niko could take Zara to the prom.

His rebelliousness was one of those qualities that had

drawn Gal to him in the first place. Back then she couldn't imagine defying her father. Dating a Troika would probably send him into fits. She was an adult now. She could do what she wanted.

Sort of. Man, she really needed to figure out a way to move out of her parents' house faster than what her librarian's salary afforded her.

"You drinking chocolate milk there, Galyna?" Max tipped his head at the few dribbles left in the bottom of Gal's martini glass.

She did love a good flirt. So why was there a funny wiggle in her tummy where her flirter should be? She couldn't seem to get it kick started. "I've graduated to chocolate martinis, thank you very much."

"Mmm. Sounds delicious. Can I try it?" Max eyeballed the glass in her hand, or maybe he was staring at her chest.

Okay, that grin he was giving her was way too sexy, and he knew it. Definitely her chest. She had dressed sexier than her usual sweater sets. Certainly not because she'd hoped to see him tonight. No, not at all. "Afraid there's not much left."

"Just enough." Max took the glass, his fingers barely brushing against hers and oh, so slowly ran the tip of his tongue over the rim and then dipped into the well, once, twice. The pink of his tongue was visible through the bottom and he swirled it around licking up every last drop.

The inside of that glass wasn't the only thing that was wet.

Her eyes must be the size of the moon tonight. Gal half coughed, half laughed.

"That is delicious. Come on over to the bar and show me how to make that." He held out his hand to her.

She almost didn't want to touch it. No doubt putting her

skin to his would be electric. She didn't need to be any more turned on by him than she already was. "I'm pretty sure your bartender can show you. He made me this one."

Someone kicked her under the table. She didn't know which sister did it though because they were both making are-you-insane faces at her.

"He's busy. Besides, I'm sure yours will be much, much sweeter." Every word out of his mouth dripped with delicious sexual innuendo.

Her hand reached out for him of its own accord. The traitor. It was in league with the butterflies in her stomach and her girly parts, which were all on team Jump Max's Bones.

The naughty look on his face said he was on that team too. He took her hand and pulled her up from her chair. She'd been right, something like electricity but more fun zipped through her sending the nicest kind of shivers along her skin. If simply touching his hand was like this, what would sex be like?

Gal mentally eye-rolled herself. It wasn't like they were gonna go into the back store room and get it on. She didn't even know where the store room was and this wasn't a porno. Max dragged her through the crowd and behind the bar. They stood side by side in the small space, so close their arms and hips touched. Max pulled down two martini glasses from the rack overhead and she felt every one of his movements down to her core.

"What's next, Galyna?" His tongue peeked out licking his bottom lip and his eyes flicked between hers and her lips. Why did it sound like he was asking a whole lot more than how to make a martini?

"Chocolate vodka, vanilla bean if you don't have that.

Chocolate liqueur, creme de cacao, cream, and chocolate syrup." If she were in her sorority house back in Michigan, she would have also dipped the rim in chocolate sprinkles, but she doubted they had any of those behind the bar.

Max grabbed both kinds of vodka without even leaving her side. Then he winked at her and sunk down, down, down her body. His hand went to her leg, using her for support. Those butterflies in her tummy burned up in the flames his touch ignited.

He slid open a cooler where all the refrigerated ingredients were kept and even the cool blast of air did nothing to lower her internal temperature. It's not like she thought he was going down there for anything other than the freaking chocolate syrup, but her libido sure didn't seem to know that.

Up came the cream, liqueur, and chocolate syrup. Kind of like he knew that's exactly where they kept all the ingredients. Gal held in a snort-laugh. Of course Max knew where everything they needed was and probably exactly how to make this drink. He owned the bar for goodness sake.

Fine. It wasn't like she didn't know they were playing a game anyway. She'd just smartened up to the rules a little better. She could do this. Max wanted to get his flirt on? Two could flirt better than one.

He took his sweet time standing back up, his eyes wandering over every single one of her curves. Gal straightened her back so by the time he got above her waist, her girls were proudly thrust forward. She wasn't disappointed by the extra sparkle in his eye as he lingered on her chest. Again.

Her hips, thighs, and butt might be bigger than was considered acceptable by main stream media and her family, but she had killer boobs. Max stared at her chest long enough that she cleared her throat. He swiped a finger across the tip of his nose and then his lips before finding his way to her eyes again.

The lust in his gaze was so powerful it seemed like his eyes were glowing with it. Gal blinked and the glow was gone, but the lust remained. "Here's everything you need, *kiska*."

Gal swallowed, not quite trusting herself to reply yet. Max leaned forward. Whoa, he was coming in for a kiss. Right here, in front of half the town. His eyes never left hers and he reached around her side, skimmed his palm along her bare arms. Her heart rate soared right up to maximum speed and at the same time she forgot how to breathe. She'd imagined kissing Max more times than she could count.

His eyes twinkled, her eyes surely matched with her own gah-gah for him sparkle. Gal parted her lips and sucked in the soft woodsy scent of him.

Max shifted and held a crystal clear martini glass right in her face. "Salt or sugar?

Gal raised one eyebrow at the bastard and sucked on her teeth. She was salty alright. "Neither. Gimme the chocolate syrup. I'll prep the glasses, you mix the drinks. I think you know what to do."

His lips pressed together in a close-mouthed grin stifling a laugh that screamed he knew exactly what he was doing. Why was she staring at his lips anyway?

She turned and grabbed the bottle of syrup and the glass out of his hand. She put all of her concentration into pouring a thick bead in a long swirl from the base to the rim, drizzling the Hershey-goodness along the edge so it dripped enticingly down the outside. A peek out of the corner of her eye showed him watching her while pouring the ingredients into the shaker. Good.

The bottle gave a satisfying splursh with her next squeeze and the chocolate covered the ends of her fingertips. "Oops."

She brought her finger up to her mouth and wiped her fourth finger clean by swiping it down the inside of her bottom lip then licking the end clean. Max knocked the shaker and had to fumble to save it. It was a wonder he didn't spill it everywhere since his eyes were locked on her mouth and fingers and not looking at the countertop at all.

Ha. All's fair in love and war. This was a little of both. Gal moved to lick her middle finger next but Max grabbed her wrist and sucked both messy fingers into his mouth. His tongue swished back and forth and then pressed against her fingers as he sucked on them. Those sparkles in his eyes went dark as midnight and she could hear his rapid breathing as if no one else existed around them.

The things that man did with his tongue had Gal's knees going weak.

"Mmm." He hummed around her fingers and the vibrations went straight through her. One by one, he popped her fingers out of his mouth, licking the tips, imitating her earlier tease, and then licked his own lips. "You are delicious."

"Uh-huh." Crap. Her voice came out breathless and wow, she sounded super-smart.

He moved even closer to her so their bodies were only centimeters apart. "I'd love to just eat you up."

The yes-please was on the tip of her tongue when his phone rang. Max's eyes narrowed and he silenced the ringer. Irritation flashed across his face and he sighed. "Duty calls, kiska. I have to go, but I will be seeing more of you."

"Okay." She sure wished she had a flirty retort to his decla-ration, but she wanted him to see more of her. Much, much more.

Max grabbed a napkin and a pen. He scribbled something on it and pressed it into her fingers. Then he kissed her palm, put one hand on the bar and leapt right over it and into the crowd. He was through the crowd and out the door before she even got her wits about her. She gave the drinks they'd mixed a shake and poured them into the glasses she'd prepped. She made her way back to the table and set the martinis down for her friends. She was riding a natural high and didn't need anything more to make her night feel good.

Heli was practically vibrating with excitement. "Holy crap. I thought you guys were going to start making out right there at the bar."

Zara nodded and picked up one of the drinks tasting it. "The way you guys were eye-sexing it up got pretty much everyone in here hot."

"Shut up. You're going to make me blush." Gal put her hands on her cheeks but there was no hiding her high color. She opened the napkin and found Max's phone number written on it, with the words, put this in your phone printed underneath it.

"Too late." Heli took the other drink and downed half of it. "So, when are you seeing him again?"

Not soon enough.

*J*ust a little dinner party. His ass. No one has a midnight dinner party just because it's a full moon. He didn't need his finely-honed wolf senses to know this was a well-laid trap.

"Mother. This isn't going to work. I see right through your matchmaking machinations."

Selena was not only the matriarch of the Troika wolf pack, she was a crafty mother who wanted her sons mated and making her grand-babies. Since Niko, the eldest wasn't here, Max had become the center of her attention. "Why, whatever do you mean, *sinochek*? I'm sure I've never had any machinations in my life."

Yeah, right. Whenever she used Russian endearments, they all knew she was planning something they wouldn't like that she was sure would be good for them. Like match making. "Your middle name is devious."

"It is not. You know very well I'm named after Tsarina Catherine." She pretended to go about her business. Which of course included sticking her nose into her three sons' business as often as possible.

So far he'd avoided her attempts to find him a nice she-wolf. This was all Niko's fault. If he hadn't gone off to Russia to serve the alpha, he'd be the one here getting set up with every other girl from here to Rochester. His brother was the future alpha of Rogue, New York. He was the one who needed a mate. Niko better bring home a nice Russian wolf beauty or their mother would have her claws in him next.

As it were, she was determined to get both Max and the youngest brother Kosta mated off before the next full moon.

Which wasn't going to happen. Max was perfectly happy to live his free and easy bachelor life chasing as many skirts as he cared to. There was only one he had any interest in lately, longer than that if he was honest, and his family would not approve.

Galyna's pretty almond-shaped eyes, dark creamy skin, and luscious curves had been driving him crazy since high school. She'd gone off to college in Michigan, stayed and got an advanced degree and he'd given up on ever seeing her again.

Until last night. He'd been given the perfect opportunity at the Sleepy Folk to taste her forbidden fruit. He could hardly believe how hot the chemistry had been between the two of them. He'd had hell to pay for not finishing his patrol of the Reserve but after seeing her walk through those woods dressed to kill, he'd taken the risk.

Selena straightened the t-shirt Max wore and brushed invisible specs of lint off his shoulder. "I've invited the alpha of Crescent and his daughter to the party. It would be simply rude of you not to come."

Great. Galyna would hate everything about Taryn Crescent. Gal was everything the wolftress wasn't. Kind, friendly, soft and curvy. And if he didn't quit thinking about her endless curves he was going to embarrass himself in front of his mother. Or worse make her think he had the hots for Taryn.

No way. "Sorry, mother, but I already have plans that night."

He didn't yet, but he would if he got his ass over to the library before the evening family story hour and asked Galyna out. He found out from Kosta that Gal had taken a job as the children's librarian in town. He suddenly found himself very interested in Winnie the Pooh and Tigger too. Tonight he was going to do something about it. Like actually ask her out on a date instead of reliving dirty fantasies of having her in his bed.

She was interested. The scent of her arousal drove his wolf insane. But she wasn't a shifter. She was human and would need wooing. Dinner definitely. A movie? No, he wanted to spend time with her, get to talk, not sit in the dark with her. Although, if he was very, very lucky they would be doing something else in the dark. In the back of his car, with her legs over his shoulders.

His mother scoffed, ending his already wild fantasy. "What? Who?"

The phone rang and Max almost howled, "I'll get it."

Thank the moon for any distraction that would move his mother off the topic of him getting mated, or who he really wanted to spend his dirty time with. He grabbed the old school handset and barely got out a hello before he was inundated with the gruff voice speaking Russian on the other end of the line.

For the rest of his life he would remember exactly where he was and what he'd been doing when he heard the catastrophic news from Russia. Each stark, guttural syllable shot him straight in the gut with pain.

Max gripped the phone too tightly and balled his other hand into a fist. "*Znayu*. I'll tell the family. *Spasiba*."

He hung up the phone, setting it very gently back onto the cradle. His mother insisted on keeping her nineteen-seventies rotary dial phone. She didn't like change very much.

He had no idea how he was going to tell her that their worlds were about to change. He swallowed, then did it again. It was taking all that he had to hold his wolf down. He wanted nothing more than to shift, throwing off all the world and go running into the reserve that backed up against his mother's house.

He and his brothers had spent more of their youth running and causing havoc in those woods than anything else. Now all three of them would never be able to do that together again.

Fuck.

He slammed his fist into the leg of the wooden stand, splintering it and causing the whole thing to fall over, telephone and all.

"Maxsim Aleksandr Troika. What is wrong with you?" His mother chastised, but with concern in her voice.

Max turned and the second his mother saw the look on his face she sat on the couch. She grabbed her throat and stared at him, begging him with her eyes not to say the words he knew he had to. "Who?"

"They said--" He couldn't say it. He couldn't even believe it. His eldest brother was dead. But it was worse than that. "Niko, he... he killed the Tzar, mom. Why would he do that?"

His mother shook her head, tears he'd never once seen from her pooled at her eyes. "I don't understand. Who is dead, your brother or the Wolf Tzar?"

He could hardly believe he had to say it. "Both."

That word rang through Max's brain over and over during the blur of the next few days, like a song he had stuck in his head that wouldn't budge no matter how hard he tried. The entire wolf shifter world was in a complete uproar and all he could think of was how it simply didn't make sense that both the alpha of all wolfkind and his brother, the future alpha of the Troika pack were dead. It couldn't be true.

He needed more information and their network of friends and allies had dried up. Every single pack had forsaken the Troikas. Some were out for vengeance.

The moonlight full-moon party turned into a pack enforcers strategic planning meeting for those in the pack who stayed loyal to the Troikas. Some had fled to the neighboring packs of Grimm and the Bay. Every man, woman, and wolf left had to be called up to run patrols around the town. Max and Kosta were no exception. They were now the leaders of those patrols.

Except when their father was. Like now. He'd always been a stern man, but now he was downright angry at anyone or anything that even looked at him funny. He certainly wasn't happy with the job Max and Kosta were doing keeping everyone safe. There had been an attack almost every night since the news of the assassination hit WolfSpace. Max had a special hate for social media these days.

"Son, pay attention. Those Grimm's will take you out with your tongue hanging from your mouth catching flies like that." His father had no patience for wool-gathering. He was a man of action if nothing else.

Max, Kosta, and his father, the alpha of the Troika pack, Piotr, were on yet another patrol to defend their home and their territory from the neighboring packs. The alphas of Grimm and the Bay saw Niko's actions as weakness and betrayal by the entire Troika pack. No wolves in Rogue, New York were safe.

"Sorry. Just tired I guess." And grieving. But none of them were allowed to show that.

"Alphas don't have the luxury of being tired. You have to be better now, Maxsim. The best. I've been too soft on you because we all relied on Niko's--" his father looked away. "You're the heir now. Start thinking and acting like an alpha because the other packs will never let us forget your brother's betrayal. We'll have to fight for every bit of our territory and the safety of the wolves of our pack for generations."

An anger he hated bubbled inside of him. How could Niko have done this to them?

No family was more loyal to the Volkov Tzars' reign than the Troikas. It was why Niko had gone all the fuck the way to Russia in the first place. Serving under Mikhail Volkov was something not every pack undertook. But Niko and Mik had gone through their first shifts together and had been tight ever since. Max would do anything to go to St. Petersburg himself to investigate the claims that his brother had fought and killed Mik. Until he did, he couldn't believe it.

Max stood up straight, wanting badly to shift to his wolf form and tear any living thing in the forest to shreds. A good alpha controlled his instincts and did what was right for the pack. He exchanged a quick glance with Kosta who'd watched the whole dressing down while leaning against a tree and looking every bit the wild child. They both knew what they had to do and would give their lives for their pack.

Kosta gave him an I'm-with-you-brother chin jerk and went back to slouching.

"Yes, sir. I know what I have to do." The responsibilities he never thought he'd have to face already weighed heavy on him.

"Good. Then do it." His father scented the air and his eyes went from human to the blue glow of his inner wolf. "Grimms. Let's show them we won't be bullied. Come on."

He shifted and took off into the Reserve. Straight for the sacred clearing they used for mating ceremonies. Shit.

Kosta shifted next, his bones and muscles cracking, and his fur bursting out of his skin. Max followed suit and ran behind the other two, protecting their six. The shift had become more painful than usual. The way his body broke itself and reformed was part of being an adult wolf-shifter, but Max welcomed it these days. He wanted that pain to remind him that he was the future alpha and would have to take on the pain of all his people.

The anguish was nothing compared to what the whole pack would feel if the Grimm's desecrated the sacred circle.

May the moonlight forever forsake them if they did.

Max stayed on the fringes in the trees, and scented the air for any of the enemy who thought to conceal themselves rather than face those they accused head on. The Grimm's used to be a proud pack, but a string of greedy alphas had changed many of them into cowards. Which was the case tonight.

No other wolves appeared in the circle, but several had been here and left puddles of piss dotted around the space. It was nothing that nature wouldn't take care of, but it was disrespectful. It was also the wolf way. The other packs felt Niko's actions the ultimate disrespect, so they were showing theirs in kind.

His father shifted and stood in the center of the clearing, hands on hips and naked as the day, peed his own circle, reclaiming the territory as his own. Max caught a different scent on the wind. Not that of any shifter where they shouldn't be, but a human.

He tore off from the clearing following his nose to the scent of honey and jasmine. The scent of Galyna. He should have warned her not to take this path again. Not now that the other packs were invading Rogue. If any wolf or man thought they could harm him or the Troikas by hurting her, they would be sorry sons of bitches. Then they would be dead.

Max's wolf wanted to howl and warn anyone else away but he controlled that instinct. She may already be frightened and he didn't want to scare her even more. The wolf-shifters in Rogue knew better than to reveal themselves to humans. It was the number one rule passed down through generations. Keep the secret, keep the pack safe.

He used every sense he had, wolf and human, to search the area and seek out any danger. His hearing, sight, and sense of smell were all much more heightened than a non-supernatural being. Galyna wouldn't even know he was there, unless he revealed himself to her. He could never do that.

Max followed her scent, while luscious as she was, also had

a tinge of frustration like burnt coffee beans about it. He
heard her voice before he saw her. The sound of her unique
lilt went straight to his groin.

"I know, I know, but my dad wouldn't let me take the car."
She paused for a moment, listening to whoever she was
talking to.

Max snuck into the underbrush about ten yards down
wind from where she was walking and scanned the area.
There were no other humans about. He didn't scent any
recent activity indicating wolves either. She rounded a bend
in the path and it was as if the moon shined brighter, the
crickets chirped a lullaby, and his heart skipped several beats.

She was so fucking beautiful. Her jeans hugged her hips in
all the places he wanted to, her top clung to her breasts in a
way that made his mouth literally water and he had to lick his
chops like a freaking lusty cartoon wolf. His wolf clawed and
growled inside of his mind, pushing him to go to her, protect
her, and most importantly make his claim on her.

There was no question that he would protect her. The
rest? Not so much. When the attacks on Rogue died down, he
would have to satisfy himself with a few dates and if he was
lucky some hot fucking sex. But beyond that, they could never
be together. His world simply did not allow wolves to mate
with humans.

"Yeah, no. He doesn't even like when I go out after dark
without a chaperone. He still thinks this is the eighteen
hundreds. I mean seriously, I'm twenty-three years old. I have
a masters degree. I think I can go out with my friends at night.
They are so old school it's killing me." She stomped right past
Max without noticing him even a little bit.

That was both good and bad. He didn't want her seeing

him, but she also needed to be more aware of her surroundings. He may not agree with her family not allowing her to go out. That would definitely interfere with his plans to ask her out. Like he had the time for that these days. But he didn't want her out walking after dark where she could be in danger. Dammit.

"No, they think I went to bed early because I was mad. I'm mad all right." She was making so much noise clomping her way down this little used path that every animal and beast in the place knew exactly where she was.

Maybe he should take her on a date to ninja school. Get her moving a little more stealthily. Max popped out of his cover and trotted down the path behind her. She was so absorbed in her rant about her parents and her phone call that he could probably go stand right in front of her and she wouldn't notice.

Gal stopped and looked to the left and then to the right. She giggled nervously. "Holy crap. Are you serious? Why didn't you say anything last week? Yes, yes, a thousand times yes. I'll start moving my stuff over in the morning."

A new scent wafted to Max's nose. Her relief and excitement was fruity and sweet. He growled soft and low, his wolf groaning at the enticing smell of her. It wanted a taste.

Gal whipped around, her eyes flitting from tree to bush to path. Max darted off the path and into the shadow of a big tree just in time. His wolf's reaction to this woman was going to get them both in trouble.

"No. I'm fine. I'll see you in like five minutes, okay? It's not that much farther to Sleepy Folk." Another pause and she laughed more genuinely this time. "Yeah get me anything with chocolate in it. Chocolate makes everything better. Even overbearing, overprotective parents' rants about finding a husband."

A husband? Over his dead body.

Gal sped up and her boots clacked onto the pavement of the parking lot at the edge of the Reserve. His family's bar was just another block away on the edge of the historic old town district. Even the Grimm pack knew better than to show up anywhere near the Troika owned businesses in town.

Hmm. If she was going to the Sleepy Folk, maybe Max would too. His father was going to be busy pissing all over the reserve for at least the next hour. He could slip away for a short time and...what?

It wasn't like he had time to hit on her. Sure, go flirt with her now and then leave her high and dry as he went back out on patrol for the rest of the night? No. When he flirted with Gal, he wanted her to be anything but dry.

He loped back into the forest and made his rounds, but everywhere he went he smelled her and it was driving him crazy. That was it. He had to get Gal Shirvan in his bed and get her out of his system so that he could concentrate on being the heir apparent to the most hated wolf pack in the world.

WEREWOLVES AREN'T REAL, RIGHT?

*G*al quickly slid the book she was reading underneath the newspaper at the desk and pretended to put the rest of the stack of children's books in order by their Dewey decimal number. They were almost all 398.45. Paranormal beings of human and semi-human form.

Ever since she'd seen that wolf in the Reserve not once, but twice she'd become obsessed. Sure, she'd started in 599.773 to look up wolves in general, but what she'd experienced didn't feel like natural behavior. It was the dumb conversation she'd had with the tweens that sent her to the folklore section of the library instead of the science shelves.

She was deep, deep down the rabbit hole of the myths and stories about werewolves and it all felt eerily real.

"Hey Miss Shirvan, whatchya reading?" Said tweens came up in their usual pack and invaded the desk. They were there for the after school snacks she kept in the desk drawer for them. At least she could distract them with food.

She pulled out a pack of chocolate covered granola bars and handed them out to the girls. "Here you go."

Tweenager number one ignored the proffered snack and pulled the corner of the book out from its hiding place. "Hey, I know this book. I read it like a hundred times in like the third grade. I was flipping obsessed with werewolves."

Tween number two clapped and squealed. "Oh my God, yaaass. Let me see."

The girls went through the entire stack, spreading them out across the desk and flipping them open to the pages with pictures. "Like, whatever. These are so fake. Werewolves are not like that at all. Haven't these people seen Twilight? They turn into wolves, not these gross half-man half-beast things. That's so 1980's."

"Dude, vampires do not sparkle. You have to read Helen Hardt's hot vamps."

"You guys, listen to the words that are coming out of my mouth. Dragons. Talk about sexy. Why are you not reading Aidy Award? She has wolf shifters too."

Well, at least these young ladies were interested in books. She couldn't get the older kids to do anything but come in for anime night.

"Miss Shirvan, you need to ditch these books and hit the romance novels. They're way better." All three girls looked at her and nodded.

Adorable.

"Okay thanks, ladies. Why don't you go pick some out for me." That would keep them busy for all of five or six minutes at least. The girls rushed off to the teen section, although one headed upstairs to adult fiction. Yikes. Did twelve-year-olds really read adult romance novels?

By the time she made the announcement that the library closed in fifteen minutes, Gal had a stack of about twenty books and three movies that were "OMG, totally not as good as the book." She had to read and report back to the girls about them all. She'd have to talk to the library director about starting a teen book club and having those three be on the advisory board. They could talk anyone into reading with their excitement for the stories.

She had to admit, she knew a lot more about wolf shifters than she had a few hours ago. The tweens were better than most research librarians she knew when it came to their encyclopedic knowledge of paranormal romance novel heroes. That more than anything had quashed her weird fantasy that some kind of supernatural beings lived in the Reserve.

Wolf shifters, indeed. So what if she'd thought that wolf's eyes had glowed when it looked at her. That had clearly been in her imagination.

Gal grabbed a couple of the top recommended books to take home, and put the rest on her cart to make a display out of for next week. The girls would be tickled by her use of their favorite topic for the rest of the library patrons.

She could dig into one soon because her walk home, now that she'd moved into Zara and Heli's third room, was even shorter than before. No more cutting through the Reserve to get to the bar on a Friday or Saturday night. She would kind of miss that. Maybe when the moon was full again she should take an evening stroll.

Every time she'd seen that wolf, she'd been on the way to the Sleepy Folk.

She hadn't seen Max there since that first night. She hadn't seen him at all since then. So much for thinking he was interested and might ask her out. Hmm. That sucked.

A shiver shook her body like someone had walked over

her grave. Her stomach sank and all the hairs on her arms and the back of her neck stood up on end. Gal put her hand over her heart. It was hammering so hard she could hear it pounding in her ears. What in the world? She got that horrible feeling someone not very nice was watching her. She spun around, but didn't see anything.

The alarm on her phone went off with the reminder to make the five minute announcement and she jumped about three feet, knocking her chair over. There was no one here. She was all alone and acting like a little girl afraid of the dark.

She took a deep breath and told herself to stop being so silly. It was almost time to go home and she was tired, that was all. Gal picked up the CB radio type handset that they used for the library's PA system. "The library will close in five minutes. If you have items you would like to check out please head toward the kiosk now. Thank you."

A yawn overtook her and she breathed in some much needed oxygen to keep her awake. She didn't mind closing on most nights because she had the last hour or so to herself and could usually take that time to prep her story time supplies for the week. She'd have to pull out one of the pre-made kits for tomorrow afternoon's program. Unless of course she did it on wolf shifters.

Yeah. A kids program on animals in their area wasn't a bad idea. Maybe there was a wildlife preservations group she could contact to see if they could bring some rehabilitated animals to the library. Not wolves of course. Well, maybe wolf puppies.

She really had wolves on the brain, because she was sure she just heard a wolf howl.

Uh, holy crap. There it went again. It sounded like it was

just outside the library. Gal rushed over to the door to shut and lock it. Patrons would still be able to get out, but nothing could come in. She did that and made the closing announcement. Just like she'd thought, no one else appeared at the book check out kiosks or the front desk.

A rustling sound came from her right and two words popped into her head in a voice that was not her own.

You're safe.

Okay. If there wasn't anyone else in the library, why was she hearing things? There were lots of stories of haunted libraries, but the Rogue branch of the Bay County library system had never had any deaths. No one on staff had mentioned any ghosts. She closed up several times a week by herself and had never seen or heard anything before.

She was being silly. Too many paranormal romance back covers with their tales of fantasy were spurring her imagination. Either someone was here with her or she'd imagined the noise.

"Hello? Is someone there? The library is closed. Time to go home." She cautiously moved toward the shelves where she'd heard the sounds. "Hello?"

They did have a small but persistent homeless population that spent a lot of time here. Maybe one of their regulars didn't have a place to go and decided to camp out. She hated to call the police, but would if she had to. First she'd see what she could do to help if that was the case.

Someone, or something, definitely scampered away. She really hoped it wasn't anyone with children.

"Time to go. You can come back in the morning if you like. We open bright and early at nine o'clock. We even have family story time at ten."

More rustling, scampering, and maybe panting? Whoever it was had put themselves in a corner now. Gal quietly pushed one of the carts full of books to be shelved into the only other escape route and then slipped around the end cap of the shelf. Someone scratched at the metal like they were climbing up.

"I'm not going to hurt you. But you do need to come out now. It's time to leave." Time for her to quit being ridiculous and get her imagination under control.

"Grrr-ruff."

A dog? It must be a stray or someone had lost their dog and it wandered in here when she wasn't looking. Poor thing. "Here poochie-poo. Come on out."

The very tippy tip end of a wet black nose emerged from the edge of the shelf. Then the end of a gray snout. A big dog then.

She squatted down and made a kissy noise. Gal held out her hand and slowly scooted closer. She didn't want to scare him. "Here, pup. Let's be friends."

The nose sniffed the air and retreated. Damn. She got down on her hands and knees. If it was skittish, being down on his level would help ease his fear of her. She'd seen that in a movie once.

"Grrr-ruff." It barked again and the next thing she saw was a gray fluffy tail with a black tip sticking out, wagging back and forth.

Good it wasn't afraid. "Do you want to go walkies? Outside?"

The tail stopped its wagging and dropped. So no to the walkies. "Is it dinner time, pooch? I'm sure I've got a granola bar around here somewhere for you. If the tweens haven't devoured them all. Not as good as a hamburger, which I could really go for. Wanna go get a hamburger with me?"

"Grr-ruff. The tail wagged again and then disappeared. She heard the same scrabble of feet running in the direction of the book cart.

Shoot. "Don't run away, poochy. No hamburger for you if you don't come back here, right now." Gal climbed back on her feet and ran after the dog. It was a blur of gray fur until it reached the cart and leapt over it so gracefully he was floating through the air.

His huge, enormous, did she say huge, furry body landed on the other side of the cart and ran like lighting down the stacks and disappeared again. Gal trotted after it, wondering if she had really seen what she thought she had. That was no dog. Even great Danes and bull mastiffs weren't as big as he was. His head had to come up to at least her chest. If she hadn't seen it leap over the cart, she would have said he was a bear.

But bears weren't gray, with thick full coats, pointed ears, and long tails. No. That pooch was no dog or bear. It was a wolf. The same one she'd seen in the Reserve. Both times she'd caught a glimpse of the animal he'd been far enough away that she had no idea how big he was. But just like before, she hadn't felt any fear. Only a weird sense of being protected.

What the hell was it doing in the library?

Before Gal made it out of the stacks she heard the clack of the metal bar to push the front door of the library open from the inside. By the time she got to the lobby area the door was just swinging back to close. Smart wolf, he let himself out. She walked over to the door anyway and pulled it the rest of the way shut. She peered out the front window for a few moments to see if she could catch sight of the wolf. He was long gone.

She really should write up an incident report. If he'd shown up when any other librarian was on duty they probably would have freaked the heck out. Gal felt a little dumb that she wasn't scared. She wasn't normally a too dumb to live kind of girl. She'd taken self-defense, she had pepper spray in her purse. She knew to yell fire to get people running to help instead of running away. And she definitely knew better than to pet strange dogs.

She opted not to write the report. It was late and no one would believe her anyway. Somehow she knew the wolf wouldn't have come in for anyone else. No sense making the entire staff at her new job think she was insane only a month after she'd started. She wanted to make friends.

Gal turned off the lights, grabbed her bag and her cell phone and went out the back staff entrance. She headed toward home, but when she got out of the parking lot, she stopped. Straight ahead was home, where she could tell Zara and Heli all about her strange experience and not have them think she needed to be committed. To the right was old town, where she could get a drink at Sleepy Folk. And maybe run into Max. To her left, past the front of the library was the Reserve. The most likely place the wolf had gone.

Gal went left.

"Hey, Galyna. I was looking for you." Max, looking a little rumpled with his shirt half-tucked in and his hair all in disarray, hollered at her. He'd come from the front of the library, the direction she was headed. "I was hoping to catch you before you closed, but I got, uh, busy with something."

"Max. Hi."

You didn't happen to see a wolf running in this direction did you? Gal didn't say that out loud. Crazy is as crazy does. Chasing after some giant wolf she'd decided was her protector was absolutely crazeballs. Max had just saved her from making a huge mistake. "I was about to go home. Want to walk me?"

"I know it's late, but do you want to grab a bite to eat with me? I'm craving hamburgers for some reason." Max ran a hand through his hair, smoothing it down.

Was he nervous? Was this a date? Gal squealed a little to herself on the inside. Using her finely honed sorority girl skills, she was cool as a cuke on the outside. "Sure. Sounds great. I was just talking to someone about getting a burger."

"Burgers it is then." He grabbed her hand and they turned to walk toward old town.

An electric warmth shot through her fingers, palm, and arm from his touch. That squeal inside a minute ago - it was nothing compared to the roar of the crowd in her head now. Her girly parts were doing the wave. Max Troika, the cool-kid crush who'd barely given her the time of day six-years ago was holding her hand. Her giddy teenage self couldn't have been any more twitterpated than she was right now.

Those sorority girl skills escaped her now and she was left with awkward teenager self scraping her mind for a topic of conversation. She would not be lame enough to comment on the weather. "Did you know there were wolves in the Reserve?"

Uh, yeah. She'd just blurted that out. Oops. She hadn't meant to say anything to anyone. She wasn't even sure she was going to discuss that with Zara and Heli. But here she was letting the word wolves fall right out of her mouth. Too late to take it back now.

Max didn't reply right away and Gal cringed. "I mean, uh, I heard that from the kids at the library. Crazy, right?"

Eye roll to herself.

Max looked at her sideways. "I have heard that. That rumor has been around town for a long time. It's where the name of the bar came from."

"Because folks are so sleepy they dreamt up wolves?" Geez. Could she sound any more of a twit?

Max laughed and that sound went straight to her girly parts. Such a sexy sound.

"No. Sleepy Folk was originally *slepoi volk*. It's Russian for blind wolf. Back in the day the bar was just called The Wolf. But when prohibition hit my, uh, family opened up the bakery and changed the name, but for the Russians in the area, they knew where to go to get their drink on. Can't take a Russian's vodka away. Law or not."

"Whoa. That's so cool. You should have that on a plaque or something at the bar. I don't think anyone knows. The prohibition part sure, but not the rest. I love etymological history like that." Gal closed her eyes and turned her head away so Max wouldn't see her embarrassment at being such a huge dork.

Because who doesn't flirt over etymology?

Max stopped walking and gave her hand a tug so she had to face him. He lifted her jaw with his knuckles and stared down at her. The light from the street lamps reflected in his eyes, made her heart skip a beat. "You're cute when you get your nerd on. I like it. You've got that sexy librarian thing down pat."

Something caught Max's attention behind her and he narrowed his eyes at the distraction. Before she got a chance to react and ask him what was back there, he looked back down at her, stared into her eyes and smiled in a way that melted her panties right out from under her skirt.

"I've always had a thing for nerdy girls." His voice had gone all low and husky.

"Then I'm your girl. I've got nerd tattooed across my rear end." Ha. Now her flirter was firing on all cylinders.

"Hmm. I like the sound of that, *kiska*." Max's eyes flicked from hers, down to her lips, and back. He slid one arm around to her back and pulled her in close, so their bodies were pressed together.

He was going to kiss her. Holy crap. He was going. to. kiss. her. Max freaking Troika, the boy, now a man, who she'd had a crush on for about a thousand million years was going to--

His lips touched hers, softly brushing over them, teasing her until she lost her breath. She sighed and wrapped her arms around his neck. All thoughts of etymology, nerds, and wolves flew right out of her head and were replaced by all the tingly fun sparkles they were lighting up in her brain.

Max slid his tongue along her bottom lip asking her to open for him. She met that challenge by nipping at his lip and pushing her tongue into his mouth to taste all he had to offer.

A low, sexy growl rumbled up from his chest.

Who needed wolves to spice up her life, when she had a Troika?

KISSES, COPS, AND CURLY FRIES

*T*he sweet taste of Galyna was a sharp contrast to the scent of her fear from earlier. Max would bet money that she didn't know three wolves from the Grimm pack had been in her library hunting her. Her instinctive sense of self-preservation had though.

Galyna's fear smelled like fruit that had gone bad and was starting to ferment. It paired perfectly with the taste of Grimm enforcer blood in his mouth. He'd taught them a lesson and sent them running back to their alpha with enough wounds to make for a good warning. What the fuck did those guys think they were doing attacking a human?

Max didn't care if he and his family had murdered the entire Volkov family for shits and giggles, humans were off limits in pack politics. The Volkov's were the biggest proponents of keeping the secret. These Grimms were risking everyone's lives by threatening a human in Rogue.

Pack and wolfkind aside, he was going to rip any other man or beast to shreds that threatened Galyna. He'd make sure everyone knew she was under his protection.

His wolf had known something was wrong tonight, and he knew better than to ignore those instincts. He'd been resisting his urge to go to the library and spend all of his time there, but something had sent him in that direction tonight anyway. There hadn't been a minute to himself all week, but he'd still had her on his mind.

Running through the Reserve he could still scent her on the walking path. He couldn't even go behind the bar at Sleepy Folk without getting a hard on. He fell into bed late each night or very early morning, exhausted, but with his hand wrapped around his cock, her soft sweet lips, or that round ass in his mind's eye.

She was driving him to distraction and tonight he'd decided to do something about it. He knew exactly what time the library closed and crossed his fingers she didn't have plans after she got off. He only had until midnight before he had to go on his patrol, but even a few hours with her would help take the edge off.

Instead of getting to make out with her in the stacks, fulfilling all his dirty librarian fantasies, he'd caught the scent of Grimms and their ill intentions wafting all around the little brick library. He'd tossed his clothes under a flowering bush and shifted into his wolf form to hunt the intruders down.

He should have gone home then, reported to his father and the teams of enforcers that the Grimms were crossing the line. He couldn't until he checked on her and made sure there weren't any more dangers waiting for her.

It all went downhill from there. He'd spoken to Gal with his mind. He hadn't even known he could do that with anyone other than other wolf-shifters. He didn't think it was even possible.

But she'd heard him alright. He was sure of that. The touch of her mind to his had felt like heaven. Now he was going to hell.

He was no better than the Grimms. He'd let her see his wolf. No humans had seen a wolf in Rogue for a hundred years. Not and lived to tell about it. Sure there were rumors, but every wolf was trained from birth to make sure it stayed that way. He was a leader now, and should be the model of what to do. Instead he was here making sure his scent was all over a human woman.

He didn't know if marking her in this way would make her more of a target or less, but there was no denying the instinctual drive from his wolf to make sure any other male knew exactly who she belonged to.

God. He was such a douchecanoe. Gal was a smart, savvy, strong independent woman. She would hate being claimed like that. He was going to do it anyway. Again and again.

Not like it was a real hardship.

Gal moaned into his mouth and pushed her tongue against his, asking him to dance with her. She was so fucking hot he was going to lose his mind and if he was really unlucky, his heart.

Nope. Worst idea ever. He needed to keep his emotions out of this. Think with his cock, sure. Think with his heart? Never.

He could stand here in the middle of the sidewalk all night kissing her, or he could take her home and kiss her all over. He really liked that plan because not only would he get her in his bed, but he'd also know exactly where she was and that she was completely safe. He broke their kiss and pressed his forehead against hers and ran his fingers through her long dark hair."Forget burgers, I'd rather eat you."

She sucked in a short gasp and licked her lips. "You're so dirty."

He couldn't tell from her whisper if that was good or bad. Please let it be good because he was going big. "I'm holding myself back trying my damndest to impress you with my restraint. Because I can't even tell you all the filthy things I've imagined us doing together. I haven't thought of anything else besides fucking you since you came into my bar that night."

"Tell me."

Oh, fuck yeah. He wondered if he could get her talking dirty too. She was so adorably prim and proper in her little sweater set and ponytail. She was the whole delicious inno-cent package minus the pearls. He might come in his pants if she told him to fuck her.

"Every night I go to bed with my hand on my cock and you on my mind. When I wake up hard as steel in the mornings, it's because I've been dreaming of you. I can't even leave the house without a tent in my pants unless I've jacked-off at least twice, usually three times."

Gal grabbed the front of his shirt, fisting it and whimpered so quietly he might not have even heard her except for his heightened wolf's hearing. The deep rich scent of her arousal was sweet like fresh baked peach pie, and it had his cock screaming at him to fulfill some of those fantasies. His wolf howled at him to mark her with more than his scent. It wanted him to bite her and mark her as his mate.

That thought, that pressure, made him back off. He'd learned long ago that allowing his beast to rule him was a dangerous path. It operated solely on instinct. Without his brain and human reasoning he was nothing more than an animal. That was no way to protect her or his pack.

He was an asshole for leaving her so needy. Sometime soon, when he wasn't operating on the adrenaline high from fighting the Grimm enforcers and having her in his arms for the first time, he'd make it up to her. If he could help it he'd never leave her unsatisfied ever again. But tonight he had to, for both their sakes.

It was the right thing to do. He needed to get a whole hell of a lot better at doing the right thing if he was ever going to be the pack alpha someday. It sucked that he had to figure that out right this second.

Max pressed a gentle and chaste kiss to her temple. He accidentally kept going and nibbled his way down to her ear and sucked her earlobe into his mouth making her moan and lose her balance. A quick mental note that she had a weak spot there that he was going to exploit very soon, and he pulled away just enough to whisper in her ear. "I want nothing more than to take you home and fuck your brains out, but we're not going to do that."

She whispered right back. "We're not?"

God, he loved that she sounded disappointed. They were going to be explosive when he did get her in bed. Max took one step away to get some needed space between them. This was already hard enough to put a stop to without her body pressed against his. "No. I like you, Gal. More than some one-night stand with an inevitably awkward morning after."

Gal dropped her arms to the side and shuffled her feet. "Oh. I, uh, I didn't, I mean, I guess we got a little carried away."

Shit. He was fucking this up, making her feel bad. "Don't for one second think I don't want to be buried so deep inside of you we both forget our names, but I'm trying to do the right thing, and if I don't stop now, I'm not going to be able to. You're too fucking sexy for me to resist for very long."

The small frown and notch of worry in her forehead that had appeared when he started talking smoothed away. She touched her lips, hiding the smile there, but it was obvious in her eyes. "That's actually really sweet. Especially since it's probably really obvious right now that you don't have to."

Phew. He took her hand and kissed her palm. "So let me seduce you the good old-fashioned way, with a burger and fries."

She looked up at him through her lashes and bit her lip in the cutest way before answering. "Make it curly fries and you're almost there."

Now they were headed back on the right track. Some flirting, later down the road sex, when he didn't have this Grimm thing hanging over his head they could do more. "What if I throw in a vanilla milkshake too?"

Gal took a couple of steps, dragging him along behind her toward town again. "Baby, I'm anything but vanilla."

Max's heart went into overdrive. His cock tried to send the alert to the rest of his body that this was about sex, but his heart wouldn't hear it. She was the girl for him and he was fucked. Not in the fun way.

He'd just fallen a little bit in love with her. Or maybe realized he already was in love. Shit.

On the way to the best late-night burger joint in Rogue, Max caught another whiff of Grimms nearby. Some of the pack were occasionally in town, because they were on the force over at the sheriff's department. He could easily differentiate scents of different wolves just like a human could tell a different person by their looks. These were two of the ones he'd chased away from the library and one of the wolves with a badge.

They weren't simply hanging around town either. They were scouting for something or someone. The path of scents had a pattern to it. A search pattern. He hadn't noticed that when he'd been in a panic that they were at the library. Here in the middle of Old Town, it was really fucking obvious. The library had been one stop on their hunt.

They weren't looking for him or any of his family. They knew exactly where to find them. The Troikas had several businesses in town including the bar, his mother's coffee shop, and the strip club Niko and Kosta had opened a few years ago. If they weren't at one of the businesses, it wasn't like their homes were a secret either. The family home had been in the same place for almost two-hundred years.

Max knew exactly what his patrol would be doing tonight. He'd set half of his wolves backtracking and the other half following the bastards. If they didn't get back to their own territory there would be hell to pay. He was already in a fighting mood, especially since he couldn't allow himself to be in a fucking mood.

"Wanna grab us a table and I'll order?"

"Yep. Don't forget my chocolate milkshake." She waved him off and grinned, heading toward the only open table at the fifties style drive-in restaurant.

Max ordered the food and eyeballed every single car sitting in the place on his way to their table. There were Grimms here, but he couldn't quite pinpoint them and that in itself worried him. They were purposefully masking their scents, disguising themselves, blending in with the humans.

He sent a quick text to Kosta asking him to meet them here. Something was brewing and it was bigger than just the other packs poking at them because of Niko and the assassination. A sheriff's car slow-rolled down the street and one of the officers stared right at him from the passenger side.

He'd already gotten a speeding ticket, three parking tickets, and ticket for a busted tail-light that certainly hadn't been broken when he'd been pulled over. His Impala was hidden away in his garage for tonight. Until things cooled down he'd be hoofing it around town. Which would probably be until hell froze over the way the Grimms were behaving.

Gal waved from their table. She was surrounded by a group of young women and when he walked up three out of the four went all giggly.

"Miss Shirvan, is this your boyfriend?" The girl asking drew the boy in the word out all sing-songy. The rest of their little gaggle went into hysterics.

"Ladies, this is my friend Max Troika."

Max gave a silent wave which only sent them into another eruption of giggles. The waitress on roller skates brought their tray of food over and Gal laughed too and waved the teens off. "Off you go. I'll report back tomorrow after school."

The gigglers moved away and Max couldn't say he wasn't relieved. He shoved Gal's milkshake toward her with an eyebrow waggle. "Don't be giving them too many juicy details, you'll make their hormones explode."

"I don't know about that. They gave me some romance novels to read today and I think they know more than I do about how to make a wolf fall in love with them."

Max choked on his burger.

What the fuck? Was there a young member of the Rogue

pack telling his or her pack mates secrets that no human should know? Maybe that's what had the Grimms doing double duty in town. He had no idea how to handle a situation like that. The days of executing wolves who let others find out about them were long gone. Mostly because the Volkov's had ingrained into their culture how taboo that was.

Shit. Niko would know exactly what to do. He'd probably have the kid dressing up as a wolf and parading around town to make a joke out of it. No, Niko would have known exactly which pups had recently hit puberty and their first shifts. He probably would have shifted with them and made them feel that their secret was too cool to share.

It's what he'd done when Max had shifted the first time. He needed to do better about becoming a real leader, and not just an enforcer.

Gal patted him on the back, laughing. "I know, crazy, right?"

He swallowed hard and took a sip of his cola. "I don't think I heard that right. Did you say fall in love with a wolf?"

"Yep. Turns out it's a very common romance novel premise. Although some of the girls would prefer to fall in love with dragons, or bears. I'm kind of fond of the idea of getting busy with a vampire."

Gal waggled her eyebrows at him. "You don't happen to have fangs, do you?"

Oh thank the moon. Max's laugh was both relief and humor. "I can think of something I'd like to nibble on."

Flirting with Gal was fun. He wished he could take her out on a real date. He could, but at risk to her life. He'd thought he could date her casually, that he could even have sex with her. She was an itch his libido really wanted to scratch and he'd go crazy wanting her, but after everything he'd seen tonight, he knew better than to think they could do anything more than have a burger together.

An alpha would know better. He was the future alpha.

Damn it. He was going to have to get his mother to set him up with some prospective mates.

After he kissed Gal one more time. Max twirled a stray wisp of hair that had escaped her perfect little pony tail around his finger and stared into her eyes. He could get lost in them. He wanted to. He couldn't.

One last kiss.

Max leaned in and Gal parted her lips. Such soft delicious lips. He was going to dream of those lips the rest of his life.

Whoop-woop-woop. Whoop. The sound of a police car's warning siren blasted almost right next to his ear. The sheriff's department car had pulled into the drive-up spot right next to their table. A deputy leaned out the passenger window and pointed at Max.

He was a Grimm pack member alright. Max caught his scent even over the burgers and Gal's sweet floral aroma. This guy had been in the Reserve.

"Gimme a sec, huh?"

"Of course. I've got these fries and a milkshake to keep me company." She dipped one of her french fries into the chocolate ice cream and took a bite. Some of the shake dribbled on her lip and Max had to keep his groan of need from escaping.

He made a promise to himself he wasn't sure he'd be able to keep, then made his way over to the car. "You're pushing your luck, Grimm. What are you doing in Rogue?"

"Making sure you Troikas aren't planning any more coup

attempts. The whole wolf world is begging us to take you boys out."

The rage Max had kept bottled up for far too long seethed under his skin and his wolf pushed at him to start a fight. "You know better than to talk pack business around humans, you douche. Shut your face and get out of my town before I decide to do something about it."

"Hey," the deputy nodded toward Gal, "I'm not the one shacking up with a juicy human. You're the one endangering us all."

AN OFFER SHE CAN'T REFUSE

Gal walked into her house on a cloud and leaned against the door behind her. Max was just on the other side. She wondered if he was leaning against the door too.

She touched her lips and re-lived their last kiss. His lips on her, his hands in her hair, tugging her tight to him. All those flutters that started in her belly, rapidly moved south. If the bulge that had been pressing against her was any indication, Max's blood was running hot below the belt too.

Then his damn phone rang again. His family sure had a tight leash on him lately. She could relate. It had been approximately three whole hours since her mom had called and left a voicemail checking in on her. It wasn't like she'd moved to Antarctica. She was on the other side of the Reserve.

In a house, with two roommates that probably wouldn't mind if she brought a man back to the house and had wild monkey sex all night long in her room.

"Gal? What are you doing?" Heli glanced out the front

window and her face lit up like a firecracker. "Oh my, you were just with Max Troika, weren't you?"

"I'm not even going to bother with the blushing and skip straight to the gushing. Yes." It was hard to keep the teeny-bopper squeal out of her voice. "He just showed up at the library and asked me to go get burgers with him, and then he kissed me, and I thought I was going to melt into a gooey mess in his arms."

Zara popped her head in from the kitchen. "Those Troika boys know how to kiss. Don't they, Heli?"

Heli pretended to be inspecting the ceiling under the scrutiny of her accusing older sister. Gal wasn't buying it for a second and a half. "Heli? What Troika brother have you been kissing?"

It's not like she thought it would be Max. He wasn't like that. Sure he had a bad boy thing going on, but he wasn't a cheater. That left Kosta and she didn't think the two of them even liked each other.

Heli shook her head vehemently. "No, no, no. It wasn't Max. I, uh, maybe had a drink with Kosta. And maybe we kissed each other's faces off. He does the cutest little growl when he gets all turned on. It's panty melting, let me tell you."

Huh. She'd had a similar panty-melting experience. "He growls? Max does that too."

Both Heli and Gal looked over at Zara and stared. Can anyone say peer pressure? Zara didn't fold. Heli folded her arms and stuck out one hip. "Come on, Zar, you have to tell us now. Did Niko do that too?"

Zara stared right back and pretended she wasn't fazed by the thought of her ex-boyfriend. But she had a tell. She'd always run a finger along her eyebrow like she had a headache when she was uncomfortable with the topic of conversation. "Like I would remember. That was a long time ago."

"Whatever. I know you spent the night with him right before he left for Russia. A year is not a long time. You know you're going to get back with him when he comes home. Everyone knows you two are destined to be together." Heli didn't waver at all. She added a cock of her hip and a smug look for emphasis.

Zara rolled her eyes. "Fine. Yes. He growls when he's turned on. It's totally hot and thank you very much for reminding me."

"Ha. I knew it." Heli pointed at Zara and winked at Gal. "They're so animalistic. I love it."

Yeah. Animalistic. Like wolves, even.

Geez. She was being so ridiculous. She just needed to watch New Moon and get this idea of wolf-shifters out of her mind. There was no such thing as supernatural beings and even if there were, they wouldn't be hanging around a town of humans like Rogue. They'd live off in the woods.

Like in the Reserve.

No.

Stop it.

Enough.

Eye roll to herself.

So, she'd seen a wolf. And Max had shown up right after that. And she'd seen him a few minutes after every time that she'd seen the wolf. None of that meant anything except she had a very active imagination.

"Are you going to see Max again?" Heli was great at deflecting.

"Are you going to see Kosta?" Gal sent it right back.

"You know, we're keeping it casual for now. He's got some family stuff going on or something." Heli waved the other two women off.

Oh. Should Gal be keeping it casual with Max? Tonight felt anything but. Kissing him had been intense and sure felt like there was something more between them than a hook-up. She really didn't want to be wrong about that feeling. She was totally going to obsess and over analyze that tonight while lying in bed. Good thing she had a bag full of romance novels to take her mind off of it.

Gal plopped her bag down on the coffee table and pulled several books out of her bags. "Did you guys know that vampires and wolf-shifters, and other paranormal beings were a huge thing in romance novels?"

Heli picked one up and turned it over to read the back cover. "Uh, duh. Where have you been, Miss Librarian."

"I'm a children's librarian, thank you very much. Not a whole lot of vampires in kids books." Although there was Dick and Jane and Vampires. For real. "I brought some home on recommendation from some of the tweens. I quite think I'd like a werewolf, oh excuse me, a wolf-shifter romance."

Gal lifted a book with a shirtless dude on the cover and growled. The girls laughed and sat down on the couch with her to look over the books. Someone else growled much more realistically than Gal had.

She glanced at Heli and Zara, but they were looking right back at her. No one was laughing now.

"Did you do that?" Gal swallowed even though her mouth had gone weirdly dry.

Heli shook her head and Zara whispered, "No."

The front door rattled and the sound of something

scraped on the outside. Something that sounded an awful lot like an animal clawing. Was the wolf back? Had it followed her home? Maybe it was hungry.

Gal put a finger to her lips to tell the girls to keep quiet and then tip-toed over to the window. She stood an inch to the right so she could peek out, but hopefully no one out there would see in. Max was long gone even though she wished he wasn't.

There was nothing at eye-level, so she dragged her view down to the sidewalk leading up to the door, even though she really didn't want to. A twinge inside of her gut told her what she was going to see. Nope. She couldn't do it. Gal glanced over her shoulder at Heli and Zara who were wide-eyed and horror movie scared.

Okay. Fine. She had to look. She pushed the curtain a little to the side and took a fast look at the sidewalk. A huge brown flash of fur popped up to the window sill and her view filled up with a mouthful of snarling teeth, dripping with saliva. The wolf growled, low and menacing.

Gal jumped back, her hand on her heart. It was beating against her chest like a woodpecker on crack.

This was not the wolf she'd seen before and she definitely did not feel that calming sense of protection. No way. As if it was a cold-blooded serial murderer, the sense of pure malevolence swirled around the beast like frigid fog.

"Gal, get back. What the hell is that thing?" Zara grabbed her upper arm and yanked her away from the window. She dragged her through the living room. "We should call animal control. Come on."

The three of them retreated to the kitchen and Zara pulled out her phone. She tapped on the keyboard and huffed. "I can't freaking find a number. I thought Google could find anything. Damn it."

Heli wrapped her arms around herself. "Its eyes. Did you see them? They were glowing. I don't think animal control is the right organization to call. We need Mulder and Scully."

They needed the grey wolf.

The scraping started up again, but this time on the back door, off the kitchen. There was no big window there. Only a little one over the sink. There was no way Gal was climbing up to look again. "Is there more than one or did it figure out where we went?"

Zara held up her phone and huffed. "I think we should call 9-1-1. I can't find any other numbers besides the line for the sheriff's office and that goes to the same place. Plus this is a freaking emergency."

Heli nodded vigorously. "Yes, call 9-1-1. Maybe they'll send hot firefighters. That is the only thing I can think of that would make me feel better. Firefighters. With chocolate."

Gal huddled in close to Heli. "You're just saying that because Kosta is on the volunteer fire brigade."

Zara punched in the numbers and held the phone up to her ear. She listened and scowled. She pulled the phone away from her ear and stared at it. "Umm, guys. The internet has gone out and I don't have a signal. I always have at least three bars here at home. Check yours."

Heli whipped her phone out of her pocket, but Gal's was in her bag in the living room. Crap. She waited for Heli to check her signal first.

Heli shook her head and held her phone out for them to see the screen. "Nothing. No service. No wifi."

Great. Gal probably didn't have a signal either. Wasn't that one of the first signs of an apocalypse? Werewolves and loss of cell phone service?

"Come with me. I'll check mine too, but I don't have a good feeling about this." They moved as a pack into the living room. Gal reached for her bag and riffled through it. Angels, help her find her damn phone.

A knock rapped against the front door and all three of them screamed. A sickly, car-salesmany voice floated in to them. "Come out, little mates. We're not going to hurt you."

Yeah, right.

"We're here to save you from the Troikas. They're going to get you girls killed if they aren't careful."

"Holy crap," Heli whispered. "What is this, a mafia shake-down? I don't like it. Not one bit. He called us mates. Are Australians even allowed in the mafia?"

Zara narrowed her eyes at the door. "Fuck off, you mafioso. You can't scare us with your bullshit. Get your own god-damned goomahs. We're taken and the boys aren't going to like hearing that you tried to scare us."

Gal and Heli stared at Zara. She rolled her eyes and whispered. "What? Like I haven't seen the Godfather? It doesn't do us any good to act frightened, even if we are."

Heli nodded, then shouted at the door, "I want you dead, I want your family dead, I want your house burned to the ground! I wanna go out in the middle o' the night and pee on your ashes!"

This time Gal and Zara stared at Heli.

"What? You said we were doing mafia movies. I figured that was better than yelling at Fredo for breaking my heart."

The three of them listened for anything else from the baddies at the door. They didn't hear any more voices. They did hear a wolf howl. Long and strong and clear as a bell, right from their front yard.

Heli and Zara jumped back, but Gal stopped them from running. She knew that howl. She recognized it as if it was a person's voice. "Wait. That's...you're not going to believe me, but that wolf is on our side."

Zara shook her head. "That's insane. Those mafia dudes must have trained that wolf as some kind of attack dog. You were just as scared as we were of it."

"That's not the same one that jumped up at the window. This one is different. It's nice." Gal crept toward the window, trying her best to see outside without being seen. Please let the gray wolf be out there. Pretty, pretty please.

Zara shook her head in a million teeny tiny no's. "What are you talking about? How do you know?"

She knew she wasn't crazy now. She hadn't imagined the giant wolf or that it was there to protect her. No way her friends were going to believe her, but bad guys and their wolf were doing their best to blow this house down. It was either sound crazy now, or later when the gray wolf saved the day and she went out to give it a treat. Like a hamburger. "Because I met it earlier tonight. At the library."

The pounding came back on the front door and scratching at the back, this time with much more urgency on both sides. "Get out here, mates. One brother isn't enough to scare us away. Niko can't save you now."

"Niko?" Zara's eyes went a bit crazy and she put her hands over her mouth. She sucked in a shaky breath and whispered through her fingers. "Gal, what the hell is going on here?"

The howl of the wolf sounded again, this time so loudly, it could have been in their living room. They all cringed at the growls and yowls of the horrific racket of animals clashing. Another howl echoed from nearby and Gal prayed it wasn't a friend of the mafiosos. The new wolf joined the fight and the din of the battle brought tears to her eyes.

She'd be sick if the grey wolf got hurt or killed because of her. "We have to do something to help. We can't simply hide in here."

"What can we do? It's not like we have any kind of weapons." Heli opened and shut drawers and cupboards. She found a paring knife, a pair of kitchen shears, and a handful of marshmallow toasting forks. "This is as close as we've got."

A loud shriek of pain and then silence stopped them all cold. Oh no. Gal grabbed the toasting forks and rushed toward the front door. She yanked it open and pointed a fork, one in each hand at nothing. There was blood streaking the front step and there were chunks of dirt and scrape marks across the lawn, but no sign of any men or animals.

"There, look." Heli pointed to the row of hedges their neighbor had across the street. The backside of both a grey wolf and a black one were disappearing into the foliage.

Zara jerked her head toward the street. The tail lights of a car speeding away really fast, especially for a quiet neighborhood like this one, were visible, but there was no way to tell what kind of car it was or see the license plates. "So what now? It seems like a moot point to call the police. Especially if those thugs are mafia."

Heli held her phone up. "I've got my signal and wifi back. It's super weird that those guys mentioned the brothers and Niko. I'm calling Kosta. If he's in the mafia there is no way he's getting in my pants."

"I guess I'll call Max too." There were too many strange

things that shouldn't even be in the same reality, much less all happening to her at the same time. The idea of putting the pieces of this puzzle together in the way they looked to be fitting now, made her stomach flip and flop.

Zara waved them all back inside, but stared off down the street again before she joined them.

Gal's phone buzzed in her hand and she answered it right away? "Max? I know you just left my house, but can you come back? Something really weird has happened."

"I'll be right there." He hung up before she could even say thanks.

"I'm going to go make some tea, or whiskey, or both. You guys want some?"

"Yeah."

"For sure."

"Okay."

It literally only took Max and Kosta two or three minutes to show up. They were probably at the bar which wasn't very far away. Gal did her best not to act like a damsel in distress, but the ups and downs of tonight had her nerves on their last hurrah and the second he walked into the living room she fell into his embrace and let a few tears fall.

"Shh. It's okay. I'm sure you could have gotten them with your s'mores forks."

Gal sniffled and raised the forks she was still clutching in her hand and waved them around. "*En garde.*"

Heli didn't seem half as rattled as Gal was by the incident. She was jabbering away to Kosta who nodded and frowned deeper with every word she said. They disappeared into the kitchen with Zara.

Gal waited until they were alone before she asked Max the

one question she was worried he would actually answer with a yes. "You know who and what was here tonight, don't you?"

He stayed silent, but held her tighter and rubbed her back.

She had to know. "Please tell me it isn't what I think it is."

"Don't worry, *lapochka*. We'll take care of it. You won't ever see or hear from them again. I swear it." He didn't elaborate on who they were. "We want the three of you to stay at my mother's tonight. She's got a serious state of the art security system that nobody is getting through. I've already called her and told her you're coming, so there's no getting out of it."

She really didn't want to sleep here tonight, and there was no way she was letting her parents know what had happened. They would freak and try to insist that she move back home. She'd really hoped Max would invite her back to his place and suspected Heli was going to Kosta's. But they couldn't leave Zara here alone. Max circumvented all of that with his proposal. It made Gal feel better that he'd anticipated what she needed. "I guess that's a good idea. I'll go tell Zara and Heli and grab a few things."

Slumber party it is. At her kind-of-boyfriend, possibly-just-a-booty-call's mother's house.

That wasn't awkward at all.

*S*elena shooed Kosta, Max, and their father out the door. "Off with you now. I'll take care of these ladies, you take care of business."

His father may be the alpha, and he the heir to becoming pack leader himself one day, but a smart wolf knew that the matriarch was the one to keep healthy and happy. Still, his mother was not the easiest woman to please and she had never liked her boys' interest in the town's girls.

Max kissed his mother on the cheek and took the opportunity to whisper to her so that Gal and the others wouldn't hear. "Remember, Zara had a thing for Niko, so don't say anything to her. We have to find a way to tell her eventually though."

Here was the part he was working up to. He swallowed and kissed his mother on the other cheek "And I know you may not approve, but I want you to know that Galyna is special to me, mother."

She didn't say anything but made sure he saw the eye-roll she'd saved especially for him when he pulled away. "I know more about what and who is more important than you think, kiddo. Now scram. We've got Magic Mike two queued up and there isn't anything a little Joe Manganiello taking his clothes off, chocolate ice cream, and mixed drinks can't fix."

Ew. "Mother."

She made a face only a mother of all boys would. "I've been living with alpha males for the last billion years. I am entitled to some girl time and you've brought me the perfect excuse."

"Hey, Mrs. Troika, would you rather have gin or vodka martinis?" Gal, already dressed in the cutest heart covered men-style pajamas he'd ever seen, held up two bottles.

"Vodka, dear. The whipped cream flavored one will go nicely with the ice cream."

"You got it." Gal turned and sashayed back toward the big TV lounge.

Yes. That's right. Sashayed, swaying her hips side to side in a way that already had his wolf howling inside. If he didn't excuse himself to join the enforcers gathering in the backyard he was going to embarrass himself in front of his mother with the giant hard-on in his pants.

Oh, the dreams he was going to have about peeling that satin shirt open and licking every square millimeter of Gal's big tits until she was squirming and begging him to get her off.

Which he wasn't going to get to do anytime soon. If ever. What he needed now was a long hard run through the woods to clear his head. What he was going to get was another fight. He was ready. The scratch marks all up and down his ribs were almost healed after the fight outside Gal's house.

Fucking pussy Grimms going for his belly instead of his throat like a real wolf.

He jogged out to the circle of men surrounding his father. They had seventy-five percent of the remaining pack enforcers here. The others were guarding the women and children gathered in safe houses around town. Normally in a brewing war like this they would have all gathered at the Troika compound, but he and Kosta had changed all the usual contingency plans when they brought the girls here.

Kosta patted his back, welcoming him into the war council. His father was pacing, his eyes already glowing a bright blue despite it being a new moon. It spoke to exactly how enraged he was. "This human matter throws a huge goddamned wrench in the works. Exactly how many women did those bastards attack tonight?"

Max's wolf's hackles rose and the muscles in his back and shoulders bunched. Gal wasn't the only human woman targeted. What the hell was the alpha of the Grimms thinking? Unless he wasn't calling the shots. Maybe some of the pack had gone lone wolf. Unlikely as it was a rare wolf who could survive long without a pack. They simply weren't built that way. Pack was everything. The alternative was unimaginable.

Several of the enforcers glanced at each other, nodded and one stepped forward. "Seven, including the three women here."

Max interjected before his father could go even more ballistic. "How did we come by this intel? Did you engage with the Grimms?"

The enforcer looked Max directly in the eye, then cast his eyes down briefly in deference. "Yes, sir. We know, because we were there when the Grimms came for them."

They were there. At midnight dark thirty, just as Max had

been at Galyna's. Because each of them were also involved with a human woman.

Shit.

His father growled. "Good job keeping the humans safe. This town had been under Troika protection for generations and never once has any of the townspeople been harmed by a wolf. We're not going to let that happen now."

Piotr hadn't made the same connection Max had. That was probably for the best for now, since he would flip his shit if he found out a bunch of the pack were coming as close as Max had to crossing a line that couldn't be uncrossed.

Wolves mated wolves. Never humans.

It wasn't fair to ask a wolf-shifter to keep a fundamental part of himself from his mate, and revealing his true nature was punishable by death.

Sure, they allowed teenagers with crushes to play and experiment with dating humans, but in the end, they all knew they would mate another wolf. The sacred clearing in the middle of the Reserve was used especially for the wolf mating ceremonies under the full-moon. Hard to ask your bride to be to have sex in front of a whole pack of wolves if she wasn't one herself.

The reminder was a painful slap upside Max's head. He could fool around with Galyna, pretend they could have something more, but deep inside he knew they couldn't. He would be alpha someday and an alpha needed a strong wolftress to rule by his side.

Something one of the Grimms had said kept nigging at his psyche. He'd called the women, little mates. He couldn't figure out why they would do that. Hopefully Gal hadn't heard it, or hadn't understood its meaning. He really didn't want to but he was going to have to ask someone with more understanding of pack politics about it.

The real question was whether he asked his father, or his mother.

Max had gotten distracted with that line of thought and the cracking and rending of bones and skin as those around him shifted into their wolves knocked him back to the reality of the situation. He needed to stop living in his head and start doing if he expected the Troika pack to follow him in the future.

He shed his clothes, dropping them amongst the other piles left by these loyal pack wolves and powered into his own shift. His bones broke and reshaped themselves, his fur burst through his skin, and Max took the pain of the transition and used it to fuel his drive to end this conflict. Peacefully or not.

The three lead enforcers ran toward the edge of the Reserve that backed up to the Troika land. They were waiting for him. They would protect him and the rest of the pack from any surprise attacks. His father and Kosta would protect the rest from behind.

Everyone knew the plan and the pack would move in complete stealth through the Reserve, across land owned by several pack members until they got into Grimm territory. Those assholes wanted a fight? The Troikas would not be sitting on their haunches waiting around for it. No they were bringing the fight to the Grimms.

They moved fast on fleet feet until twenty-some odd wolves surrounded the Bay County Sheriff Department's brick building. Kosta and Max approached the front door and their father took up position so that any wolf trying to flee would meet their fate with him.

Kosta shifted and pulled the heavy metal door open. He sauntered in, naked as the day is long, with Max at his side protecting his brother's more fragile form with bared teeth and claws that clacked on the linoleum floor. The small foyer opened up to a reception area with a smattering of deputies and other personnel sitting at desks behind. The sheriff, who was the Grimm's top enforcer had an office off to one side.

He leaned against the doorframe, his arms crossed, one foot propped up on a nearby chair and a toothpick hanging from his mouth. "What are you boys doing here? I could arrest you for indecent exposure and put your puppy there in the pound."

Max growled, but kept quiet waiting for Kosta to lay out the rules. "Tell your humans to leave. We're not here to hurt them."

The sheriff walked over to a young man in a uniform and put one hand on his shoulder, but without taking his eyes off Kosta and Max. "Reagan. You want to leave?"

"No sir. Not unless you tell me to, sir." The young man looked at the floor while he spoke.

Max sniffed the air. Reagan was definitely human. He wasn't scared. No, what Max smelled was subservience. Submission the man did not like giving. It was tainted with the wet earthy scent of resignation.

A young woman, mid twenties, wearing a floral dress stood next to a copy machine. The sheriff jerked his chin at her and she came running over and knelt down in front of the man. Her hands rested on her thighs and her eyes were facing down. The sheriff ran his hand over her hair.

"See boys, we've decided to do things differently here in Grimm. Our humans know we are the superior race and they submit to our rule like the good little pets they are. Isn't that right, little mate?" He lifted the girl's head by her chin so she had to stare at her own nose to avoid looking him in the eye. Then he spit in her face.

She didn't even flinch. Her scent betrayed nothing of her feelings. All Max could smell on her was the sheriff. The fuck-tard had taken this human and turned her into some kind of damned Stockholm syndrome slave.

Max and Kosta shared a look that, without words, asked each other what the fuck?

Kosta shook his head and pointed at the sheriff. "You're breaking wolf law that has been in place for a long time, Grimm."

The sheriff laughed and stalked across the room. The irises of his eyes glowed with the wolf inside of him wanting to come out. "The Troikas are the reason we can. You high and mighty assholes assassinated the last thing standing in the way. There are a lot more of us that are tired of hiding who and what we are. The last Volkov Tzar and his outdated rules can't stop us from taking what is right-fully ours now."

Max growled and stepped forward to meet the degenerate. Wolves had lived among humans peacefully for centuries and if he and his pack didn't stop this pack from exposing them all, peace would be destroyed. Both humans and wolves would be hunted once again.

Wolves were stronger, faster, and had the advantage of their canine senses even when in human form. But their numbers were dwindling. Each generation had to go farther afield to avoid inbreeding and some never found a mate. They would be hunted to extinction.

Any fool who thought their gift made them superior was wrong.

"Join us, Troikas. There's plenty of women for two young bloods like yourselves, human and wolftresses. We'll take over this town, then the next, and the next. Wolves across the country will join in our revolution and we'll no longer have to hide in the tiny tracks of forest and open space. Wolves will reign and the name Grimm will be feared and respected by them all."

Well, fuck a plucked duck. Not only did they have to defend their territory from these dickheads, they were going to have to do a crap ton of clean-up and find out exactly how many humans the Grimm's had revealed themselves too. What a shit show.

Max expected Kosta to refute this blathering idiot head on. He was oddly quiet. Max answered for them all with a series of gruff barks and a howl, which was the signal for the rest of the pack to attack.

"Join us, or die. Join us or your women will be the first we take." Instead of shifting, the sheriff pulled out his gun and aimed it at Max. "Actually, we're going to take your human mates anyway."

The sheriff fired and Kosta jumped in front of Max. He shifted in mid-flight through the air and the bullets caught him square in the haunches. He barked out in pain and went skidding across the dingy floor, blood smearing the ground.

A few mere bullets couldn't hurt a shifter. Max's heart stuttered a bit for a second anyway at his brother's sacrifice for him. You didn't have to do that, little brother.

You're the heir now. I did in fact have to. Now get the bastard while I get these damn things out of me. Within seconds the bullets were pushed out of his body by his wolf's healing abilities and clattered to the ground.

A stream of Troika wolves poured into the building and the Grimm wolves, all six in the office area, burst through their clothes and shifted into their wolves too. The humans, all except the young lady, scattered or took cover. What was wrong with that girl?

Max jumped through the air toward the russet wolf that the sheriff had transformed into. His hulking body was bigger than Max's and he met the fight with teeth and claws bared. He snapped his jaw down on Max's shoulder, tearing at the muscles, trying to get him to fall to the ground.

Trying to get Max to submit.

A power deep inside of him, that he'd never needed to call on before, rose up and he kicked the other wolf away. It didn't take him long to jump on his enemy's back and take him down. A lust for blood and to protect what was his pulsed through him and Max tore the other wolf's throat out.

He howled, a new intense tone in his bay to the moon. The fighting around them stopped and the Grimm wolves ran, retreating from the fight. Another howl, matching his own sounded outside.

His father's voice filtered through the blood rage in him. The alpha power in you has scared the cowards away. Good job, son. We're going in pursuit.

Max sat and panted, cooling his body and gathering his thoughts back to normal. He couldn't. His father had never once given him any sort of praise. That was always reserved for Niko.

Kosta padded up to him, glanced down at the dead and

mangled wolf at their feet, and sat too. Guess you're the golden child now, dickwad.

Kosta shifted again into human form, signaling to the others it was safe to do the same. The humans came out of hiding, and a few brought the enforcers blankets and bits of clothing to cover themselves. All except the girl. She hadn't moved throughout the entire fight.

Max didn't want to scare her so he too shifted, even though it meant losing communication with his father. He could switch back again later to find out what, if anything, else needed to be done.

The man who'd been questioned before rushed over with a pair of sweatpants in his hand. "We keep a whole stock of these around for, uh, shifting emergencies."

Max slipped the sweats on and carefully approached the young woman. He squatted down beside her and clasped his hands in front of him so she would know he wouldn't touch her without her permission. "You're safe now. He's dead and you're free from his rule over you. Do you understand?"

She breathed in, she breathed out, and nothing more or less.

Max glanced over at Reagan. 'What's her name?"

"Kiara, Kiara Cross. But before all this, I, I mean, we called her Key." Reagan was trying real hard not to look at the girl.

"Key." Max moved so he was in front of her. "Can you look at me?"

Nothing.

"He trained her not to respond to anyone but him." Reagan glared down at the body of the wolf bleeding on the floor and spit on it. "Fucker."

Kosta approached very slowly and came only close enough

so he could speak in a normal voice to Max. "Use your alpha voice. It might snap her out of it."

Shit. Max hadn't even realized he had an alpha voice now. His father had one, and Niko too. Someday Niko's first born would have had one too. No command given by an alpha could be ignored by a member of the pack. "I don't think it will do anything. She isn't pack. She isn't even a wolf."

Reagan moved closer too and for the first time looked at Key. There was a lot of pain in his gaze and scent. "She is. He mated her under the last full moon."

"Holy fuck. Did he mark her?"

"I don't know what that means."

"Key, I'm going to touch you, move your shirt to the side. Don't be afraid, I only need to see something." Max gently pushed the collar of her shirt, exposing the skin on her neck and shoulder. A crude black symbol of a wolf marred her skin. Both above and below it were the healed bite marks of a wolf.

Max's own wolf rose up inside, pushing to the surface, its instincts to keep one of its own protected too strong to hold down. His own teeth extended, his claws erupted from his fingers, and fur pushed through his skin. How could a wolf do this to a human?

Biting and marking a human was wolfkind's darkest, deepest taboo. There were legends and rumors about what happened to bitten humans. It's where the folklore of the werewolf had come from in the first place. No one alive today truly knew what happened because no human had been bitten by a wolf shifter in hundreds, maybe thousands, of years. She might be a monster like the stories claimed.

Max sucked in a long, calming breath and got his wolf

back under control. He pulled on the might that the partial shift had given him and put the power of the alpha into his voice. "Rise, Kiana. I have defeated your mate and claim you for my pack. You are Troika now."

Key blinked and tipped her head to the side like she was awakening from a deep meditation. The blue glow of a Troika wolf shined in her eyes. She glanced over at the dead wolf, then at Max.

The blue light around her irises grew until the wolf inside of her overtook all the color, the pupils, and the whites of her eyes.

Max and Kosta surrounded her, in case she couldn't control the shift or the wolf. Kosta shook his head. "I've never seen any wolf's eyes do that. What the hell?"

Key tipped her head back and howled with the voice of a wolftress, but her bones did not break, her skin did not split. She remained human, except for those damn eerie glowing eyes. She growled low and then a haunting voice, only partially human said, "A Dragon, a Witch, and a Wolf walk into a bar."

*G*al shifted from foot to foot standing on the grass in front of the house she shared with Heli and Zara. Max and Kosta were doing a check of the perimeter and then inside to make sure there weren't any surprises waiting. They both looked exhausted and Gal couldn't help but wonder if they'd gone out looking for a fight after they dropped her and the sisters off at their mother's house last night. Max didn't appear to have any visible injuries. Although Kosta had a barely noticeable limp. Did they take care of the problem?

Wondering how they might have done that gave her a shiver. She couldn't even blame it on the early morning air. It was two o'clock in the afternoon and the early summer day was nice and warm.

She hefted up the bag with her new pajamas, and the full set of high-end spa products Selena Troika had foisted onto each of them last night. It was really interesting that she had all these clothes and supplies all ready to go. Like she ran a women's shelter out of her living room.

Gal had taken a peek in the hall closet and it was filled with small packs of clothing, toiletries, and other sundries that someone who had to leave their home in a hurry might need. There had been packets of smaller clothing with coloring books and other toys for kids too. But none for men.

They hadn't slept on couches or the floor like she'd expected. Nope. Selena had fancy camping cots that were more comfortable than Gal's own bed at home, a mountain of pillows and blankets, and even sleep masks and earplugs ready for them. Selena had done everything she possibly could to make the three women who'd arrived freaked out feel welcome. They'd had drinks, snacks, movies, giggles, and girl talk until about three in the morning. The reception and the evening couldn't have been any better of a cure for the fears, uncertainties, and spikes of adrenaline.

The four of them laughed, they'd drank a little too much, and they'd eaten an entire ice cream shop's worth of banana splits. When the sugar rush and adrenaline crashes came, they slept. Hard.

This morning when they'd woken up to the scent of cinnamon rolls, coffee and bloody marys. Selena had beautiful and expensive outfits picked out for each of them. Just the bra and panties, matching ones, were more expensive than pretty much the entirety of Gal's closet.

Standing in front of the house, out on the sidewalk with Heli and Zara, she was sure the neighbors were staring. At least one busy-body across the street had peeked through their blinds.

"Dude, you saw the inside of their house and these fricking expensive outfits she had ready for us." Heli held up her arm, waving the flowing sleeve of a designer shirt, and the jingle of a pretty little charm bracelet. That is mafia money. I'm telling you."

She wasn't wrong. This was mafia type money. But there was no way the Troikas were involved in organized crime. Max had honor, he believed in right and wrong. He wouldn't purposefully hurt people for money. No way. She wouldn't believe that of him.

Gal was still putting the pieces of the Max puzzle together in her head. Something wasn't adding up with him and the rest of his family. She shrugged, not ready to commit to anything. Or sound too crazy. "Maybe the bar does really well."

Heli scoffed. "Kosta runs a strip club. Tell me that's not a mafia front."

Zara poked her sister in the arm. "I think you just like the thought of being a mafia wife."

Zara was the only one of them who'd been in the Troikas home before. She'd stayed reserved and quiet through the evening, but hadn't seemed uncomfortable. Selena had a way of making anyone feel welcome and like they were the most important thing to her in the world in that moment. If she'd ever had a problem with Zara dating her eldest son, no one would ever know.

Heli laughed and poked Zara right back. "No way. Leopard print, big hair, and big nails are not my style. Besides, I don't even have a Jersey or Italian accent."

"Neither does Kosta. They're Russian." Zara's tone laid the no-duh on thick.

Even with the weird and scary events of last night,Gal thanked her lucky stars she'd moved in with the sisters. It was moments like these where she wished she'd had an understanding sibling to confide in and poke. Her brother was way more like her dad and thought going off to college was a waste of time. For women in general, not just her.

Heli gave them both the whatever look. "Then it's the Russian mafia. That's a thing, right?"

Max opened the front door and waved them into the house. Even tired, wearing sweatpants and an old Sleepy Folk t-shirt, his looks took her breath away. It wasn't just how handsome he was, but more the way he watched her, like he couldn't tear his eyes away. He had that same charm his mother did, but with a sexy edge to it. When it was aimed at her, she wanted to laugh, and cry at the same time.

The three of them moved toward the house so their conspiracy theorizing would have to go on hold until later. Gal had to get one last rebuttal in. "It is, but I still don't think any of them are baddies. There would be rumors in town, everyone would know, but not really. Trust me, the moms at story time are worse than the Enquirer for gossipy stories and I would have heard something."

When they got inside Heli and Kosta disappeared into her bedroom before anyone could even say anything. Zara rolled her eyes. "I think I'm going to take a nap. Thanks for helping us out last night, Max. Say hi to your brother for me the next time you talk to him."

Something flashed across Max's eyes at Zara's request, but he hid it with a quick smile. "No problem. I'm sorry those guys made trouble for you. Sleep well."

Zara went down the hall which left Gal and Max all alone. With nothing to do. Zara shut her door and the second the latch clicked indicating it was closed all the way, Max pulled Gal into his arms and mashed his mouth down on hers.

This kiss was nothing like the ones they'd shared last night. He was intense and needy, demanding even. He cupped her head in one hand and grabbed her ass with the other, yanking her whole body tight to his. His tongue swept along her lips and pushed into her mouth. Gal came right back at him slipping her tongue along his and wrapped her ankle around the back of his calf.

Max groaned and kneaded her butt with those big strong hands of his. His lips moved over hers, their teeth clacking together at the force of their rapidly increasing need for each other.

Pure need. She needed to know he was okay, that she was. She needed him to reassure her that everything was going to be okay, and she absolutely needed him to need her.

Gal pushed her hands up under his shirt, shoving it up, loving the feel of his hot skin under her fingers. Max broke their kiss for only the second it took him to cross his arms and pull the t-shirt off and throw it onto the couch.

Oh, the couch. Good idea. She put her palms on Max's pecs, gave them a quick squeeze, and small shove to get him to back up and sit on the couch for this post battle adrenaline make-out session. He didn't even budge. Geez, he was strong. She put a little muscle behind her shove and he still didn't move.

Max looked down at her hands and then back at her. "Babe, not that I don't love your hands on me, but what are you trying to do?"(see note)

She huffed and really put some force behind her push this time. Nothing. "I'm trying to get you to sit down on the couch. But you're like made out of stone, or adamantium, or I don't know. What are you? Like son of Kal-El or something?"

Max smiled down at her and booped her right on the nose. "Aww, my adorable little nerdy girl. I promise, I'm of this Earth."

"Did you just boop me on the nose?" She wrinkled said nose up at him.

"Yes. Now come here and let me boop you on other places. After last night, I'd really like to know that every single part of you is unharmed." Max lifted her up by the waist, plopped down on the couch and placed her straddling his lap, with her boobs right up in his face.

She squirmed, a little uncomfortable at the idea that she was going to squish his junk if she sat down at all. "This is not exactly what I meant."

"It's perfect." His phone rang. That same damn tone that meant his father was calling. Max dropped his head back onto the couch. "Fuck me."

Oh no. Not this time. His dad could wait. Mafia or no, Max needed some down time. "Leave it. Call him back."

He groaned. "I can't."

Wanna bet?

"What about if I do this?" She pulled the fancy new shirt off and tossed it over her shoulder. Her brand-new expensive bra followed. Gal cupped her breasts, rubbed her hands over them in tantalizing circles, and twirled her nipples between her fingers until they went hard.

"Holy fuck. I'll call him back." Max shoved Gal's hands aside and replaced them with his own. "You have no idea how many times I've dreamed of doing exactly this."

Had he? He probably didn't mean that literally, but it boosted her confidence nonetheless. "Talk dirty to me, Max."

Yep, that had popped out of her mouth. She wasn't

normally a tiger in the sack. She did just fine, but she wasn't exactly one to ask for what she wanted. She'd always kind of hoped the guy would figure it out. It wasn't like it was hard. Being here with Max was so much hotter and yet more comfortable than any other sexual experiences she'd had in college.

"You like that, do you, my dirty girl? Then let me tell you exactly what I've been dreaming of." He rolled one nipple, pinching it, making her whimper. "First I take these tight, hard nipples and I suck on each of them, licking and tasting and teasing until you're moaning beneath me."

He lapped at one nipple and pinched the other one at the same time. Then he switched, giving her only the tiniest preview of his dream.

"Mmm-hmm. Tell me more."

"Just how dirty do you want me to get, kiska? Do you want to hear about how I wake up so goddamn hard after dreaming about fucking these lush tits? Do you want to know that I fantasize in the shower about pushing my cock between them while you're on your knees, holding them together? Because if you do, then you'll find out that I come calling your name imagining you sucking my head into your mouth with every thrust."

Holy fantasy, Batman.

"I, uh,--" Yes, she wanted to know all of that and more, so, so, so much more.

"Fuck, I'm not looking, I'm covering my eyes. But dad is freaking the fuck out that you didn't answer your phone and thinks you're dead. We have to go. Now." Kosta stood an inch into the living room, one hand over his eyes, and the other tugging his pants up.

Gal dropped down and fell sideways onto the couch, covering her chest with her hands. That put her into the awkward position of her bum across Max's lap, straight up. As if she was waiting for a spanking. If she wasn't already flushed, she'd be turning fifty shades of pink.

Max placed the palm of his hand on her derriere and held her in place. "Fine. Give us a minute. Dad can wait one goddamn minute."

"I'll be outside." Kosta whizzed through the living room.

Gal buried her face in the couch cushion until she heard the door open and shut. "You can remove your hand now. I need my shirt."

"Not quite yet. I like you in exactly this position and I want to remember this moment for the rest of a night that is going to be very trying." Max's hand moved across her butt, squeezing one cheek and continued down to her thigh. His fingers dipped in between her legs. "The scent of your arousal is intoxicating."

Gal wiggled to get away. Her scent? He might sound turned on but she was sure he was politely telling her she needed to bathe. "I think your minute is up and apparently I need to go take a shower."

Max did not let her up. Nor did he react to her embarrassment at him telling her she smelled. "I want the scent of you on me tonight. Given a little more time I could have had you riding my fingers while I sucked on your tits. You're wet and I'm dying to touch you, taste you."

"Maxy, I do not relish the ass-chewing we're both getting when we get... uh... home. You're not the only one leaving with blue balls, let's go." Kosta shouted from the front porch in a stage whisper. The neighbors were probably cursing him.

"I will be there in a fucking minute." Max's words came out on a low growl.

A growl that had her stomach and pussy fluttering. She did not have a thing for angry guys, but Max with a mad-on was like a damn aphrodisiac. The pure dominance in his voice had her wondering if she didn't have a little bit of a kink.

He sighed and gave her butt a smack. "Up you go, kiska. I have to go, but when you're taking your shower, I want you thinking about every word of that fantasy."

Gal rolled off his lap, which landed her on her knees on the floor right between his legs. Neither of them had gotten as far as unbuttoning pants, but the huge bulge at the front of his jeans was begging to be let out. She placed a hand on each of his thighs. "If you stayed we could live out your fantasy right now."

"Galyna, you're killing me. I'm this close to betraying my entire family to stay here and fuck you until we both forget our names."

She leaned forward and ran her tongue across his entirely too lickable abs and reveled in his deep groan. "I know you can't stay. That was to give you incentive to come back later."

"I honestly don't know if I can. There's some serious shit brewing that I need to keep as far away from you as I can. But I swear to the moon and back, I will try my best to be in your bed as soon as I possibly can. If I'm not back by sunrise..." Max stood and pulled her up with him. He grabbed her head and took her lips in a hard, needy kiss, pushing his tongue in and out, fucking her mouth, making her breathless. "I want you to slide your fingers between your wet pussy lips and imagine it's me, my tongue lapping at your clit, until you come calling my name."

Oh, she wasn't waiting until morning to do that.

Max rubbed his thumb across her lips. "I'll be back. I don't know when, but I will. I swear it."

"Go. Before you get in trouble, or I drag you to my room and tie you to my bed." Gal finished her statement with a nip to his thumb.

Max's already dark eyes sparkled and his eyelids dropped so his gaze was sultry and hooded. "Saying something like that does not exactly make me want to leave, darlin'."

"Because I don't exactly want you to leave. But I get that you have to deal with the demands of the family. So go already, so you can come back."

Max searched her eyes for another minute longer. Did he get when she said the family, she meant mafia or whatever the Troikas were into? Probably. He was a smart guy, and when the time was right, he'd tell her what their business really pertained to and how she and the sisters fit into the so called serious shit he was trying to protect her from.

He nodded, scooped up his shirt, and walked out the front door, with one last longing look back at her.

Phew. She fanned herself. Man, he made her hot. She grabbed her clothes off the floor and headed down the hall to take that shower. A very cold one.

The giddiness that tingled inside of her from head to toe was more than the almost sex. Max's attention was so much more than she was used to. The guys in her past were mostly the nerdy type, the kind who knew that human sexuality was filed under 306.7 or 612.6 under the Dewey Decimal system at the library and had probably studied said texts to prepare to have sex the first time.

Not Max. He knew what he was doing. He was probably

the sexiest virgin ever. She'd been a slightly awkward virgin who had worked really hard to hide her lumps and jiggles in the dark.

Max's complete and utter lust for her had given her a boost to her confidence she hadn't even realized she needed. It was so easy to be confident with him. She couldn't imagine having asked him to talk dirty, or said anything about tying him to her bed with anyone else. He was so easy to be herself around. Mostly because he seemed to not only like her real self, but was turned on by it.

That was not something she had any experience with and what she needed was some serious girl talk to analyze the crap out of everything. She took her shower and a short nap, really grateful this was her weekend off. Monday was going to come way too fast.

Around seven in the evening she'd waited as long as she could to knock on Zara and Heli's doors. She was prepared to offer drinks, take-out, or ice cream in exchange for getting their butts out of bed to talk men.

Heli answered the knock on the first try. "Buy me Thai food and I'll happily dole out the Troika men talk over noodles all night. I could use some advice myself. What goes with pad thai? Chardonnay?"

"I don't know." Gal laughed. She stepped across the hall to knock on Zara's door. "But your sister might. Let's see if she's in. I have a five dollar credit at Doordash or UberEats, I can't remem--"

Zara's door swung open when Gal rapped on it. Zara wasn't in there.

"Zara?" Maybe she'd gone to take a shower? Gal didn't hear

any running water. She turned back to Heli. "She didn't have to work did she?"

"No. The center is closed on the weekends." Heli stuck her head into Zara's room. "She was exhausted too. Said she was probably going to be out for the night."

"Zara," Gal called toward the kitchen and living room.

"Gal. Look." Heli pointed to Zara's bedroom window. The curtains fluttered in the evening breeze. "She never opens that window. There's no screen and the bugs get in. Mom always says they bite her more because she's so sweet."

The two of them crossed the room and pulled the curtains away. A whole swarm of mosquitos hung in the air not three feet away. Gal stuck her head out to look into the back yard. The grass and dirt at the side of the house had been disturbed.

Her heart jumped into her throat, beating hard enough to choke her. "Heli. Look."

Scratch marks similar to what the wolves had left in the front yard were in the dirt under the window sill. Gal stepped back and when she removed her hand from the metal something stuck to her fingers. A small smear of rusty brownish red smeared when she touched it. "I think this is blood."

BAD WOLF

"If it is a war they want, it's war they'll get." Max's father prowled in huge figure eights through the sacred circle in the clearing. He had gathered all the enforcers again tonight. Even though most of them were going on little to no sleep as Max and Kosta were, the lot of them filled the woods with their warrior's energy.

The calm before the storm, and their father was whipping up a tempest with his pre-game speech.

Last night's fight hadn't been the only one. Packs around the world were lining up, taking sides, and battling for territory and dominance. Without a strong Tzar at the helm, all the riff raff, the lone wolves, and the scariest of all, the one-bloods, had come out of their hiding places and wreaked havoc on good law-abiding wolf-shifters around the world.

Without Mic Volkov and his iron fist of enforcers, without a clear heir to his throne, and without consequences, wolves around the world were revolting against the long-held rules, laws, and customs of their kind.

Wolfspace was exploding with reports of pack wars, each

worse than the next. If someone didn't take control soon, their entire species would be exposed.

Which is exactly what the Grimm pack, and others wanted.

"The Troikas will take control of the packs in the Northeast. It will be a hard battle to convince many of the alphas and the wolves under their protection that we are not the enemy. Many know us and have been in contact to say they stand with us." Piotr stopped and stared into the eyes of each enforcer, saving Kosta and Max for last. "Many more have declared us outlaws. That is where we must take the battle first."

Grumbles and growls of approval sounded from all around the clearing. The wolves who remained after Mic and Niko's deaths were loyal to the end. Max glanced at the band of brothers he was proud to call his pack. He would give his life to protect theirs, and they his.

He only hoped it wouldn't come to that. They all had a lot more living to do.

Piotr continued on with his plan. "I will go to the largest packs myself, and am sending the strongest of you out as emissaries to the rest. You must convince many angry alphas to join us. You must show them that a united front is the only way to survive the coming war."

Aleksei, a huge mountain of a man, and an even bigger wolf, stepped out of the ranks and into the path of Piotr's march. "Who will defend and protect our families, this town, if we are out begging for fealty from our rivals?"

Piotr did not have a quick reply as Max expected. In fact, he said nothing. What was he waiting for?

This was the part where Niko would have stepped up and

given a rousing speech. Whipping the enforcers into a frenzy and convincing them they were all invincible.

Max was not Niko.

It was time the pack understood that.

He stepped into the clearing to face Aleksei. He was one of the six who had been with a human woman last night. His fear was the same as Max's own. Who would protect the fragile human women they both cared so much about? "I will. I swear to you, and all of the Troika pack, that I will protect those you love with my life. It is my right and duty as heir to the alpha."

A similar round of growls moved through the enforcers. This time with a marked relief. Even the scent in the clearing changed, the edge of smoky tension lifted. They'd been waiting for him to step into his place at the right hand of his father.

This was his first step.

His father nodded at him, the second time in as many days he'd gotten the old man's approval. Finally he was doing something right.

Piotr paced again targeting the enforcers who would be tasked with this mission under his glowing stare. "None of you have long to complete your tasks. The full moon begins in four days. We will have a mating ceremony on the third and final night. If you can find mates among the packs to cement our alliances, bring them here in no more than a week. A mate will make you stronger and will be your rock in these difficult times. Choose wisely."

The biggest and baddest of the Troika enforcers, ten of them, filed forward and received their assignments. A few, mostly the ones he suspected all had human girl friends stopped and shook his hand after they found out their doom. Once they were sent off, the enforcers left behind drew together in small groups.

These shifters hadn't been chosen for the A-team, but they were about to become Max's new elites. They weren't as big and burly as men like Aleksei, but they were warriors just the same. Max had never been as big as Niko either. If he could step into shoes that big, these men could too.

Piotr joined his sons, pulling them into a big bear hug. "Aw, my boys. You two must keep the pack safe and running like the well oiled machine the rest of the packs need to think we are. I will bring back reinforcements and a mate for each of you."

Great. "Don't worry about mates for us, sir. It's more important to get those packs on our side."

Piotr clapped both brothers on the back. "How do you think I'm going to get them to agree? It's why I raised such handsome sons. I always knew pack alliances would make us strong."

He shifted into a his great tri-colored wolf and howled at the near full moon. Take care of this town and your mother. I'll be back.

Kosta waited a full three-minutes before he mimicked his father with a pretty good Arnold Schwarzenegger impression. "I'll be back."

"Yeah, and apparently with mates for us." The idea had Max's stomach churning and his thoughts turning back to Gal. Which was stupid because he couldn't mate with her. She was a human. He was a wolf.

Or rather, it hadn't been done under the reign of the Volkov Tzars. Before that he couldn't say. The law must have come from somewhere and sometime when a wolf and a human had done enough stupid shit to create the need for the ban in the first place.

It would be so easy to do a whole lot of stupid shit with Gal invading his thoughts every second of the day.

"Fuck that." Kosta waved him off. "Roshambo with me to see who gets to go harass the Grimms and who gets to play nursemaid to mom and that poor girl we took off those dumbasses last night."

Max didn't think either was a good idea. He played the game anyway. "Rock, paper, scissors."

Kosta threw a rock. He always did, without fail. Max and Niko had made a pact when they were young and stuck babysitting to never reveal that observation to their little brother. "Damn it. I don't know why I even play with you. You always win."

Games were the perfect enticement to most any wolf. They were all competitive by nature and their own parents had turned everything from cleaning their rooms to learning to shift into a game for them. It was the perfect way to get the remaining enforcers skills up to snuff and turn their rote routine of patrols around town into an interesting training. "Remember when mom used to take us out to the Reserve and play hide and seek in wolf form?"

"No." Kosta folded his arms and pulled a very put upon expression. "Don't make me do it."

"Take half of our remaining enforcers. I want their stealth skills so solid I don't hear or smell them coming. I'll take the others. First entire team to get to the Sheriff's department unseen by anyone, humans or wolves, and especially Grimm pack enforcers, wins."

"Fine. But I'm hiding at Heli's and you owe them all a round at Sleepy Folk when we're done."

"Heli doesn't live in the Reserve or anywhere near the Bay County Sheriff's department so she's off limits for this training exercise and if you can sneak up on me beers are on the house."

"I'm kidding. Don't go getting all serious on me just because you're the heir now. Fuck, dude. That's what Niko did and look how that turned out."

Before Max could smack his brother upside the head, Kosta shifted into his dark black wolf and bounded over to pick his team of wolves for the game. What a douche.

Max shifted into his big grey wolf and gave the instructions for the game to the enforcers on his team. The team that would win. As he guessed, the wolves went from upset they weren't picked to go on the alpha's mission to excited with a renewed energy. He knew for most of them that last night's fight was the first serious pack battle they'd been in. This would blow off steam and allow him to make sure the wolves and people of Rogue were safe and protected.

He howled signaling the start and his hunting pack ran into the forest, disappearing into the night. He nipped at a few of his wolves to get them back into hiding, but near the west edge of the Reserve something not quite right caught his attention. A spicy floral scent that should not be there.

Gal.

Scared and in trouble.

Max signaled to the closest wolf to him. Continue on. I'll catch up. I need to check something out. Win the game and not only are beers on me, so are burgers.

He waited until the pack was well on their way and

pivoted to bolt in the direction of Gal's scent. Even with the power of his wolf, his lungs, heart, and muscles were pushed to the max in his speed to get to her. It didn't take him long to find her hurrying along the main path through the reserve, holding her side, little beads of sweat dripping from her hairline.

"Max? Can you hear me? Max? I need you. Please be out here."

Fuck. Why would she think he'd be in the Reserve after dark? The park closed at dusk, specifically to give the wolves a chance to run free for a while in a safe space. The pack did a good job of scaring away any rebellious teenagers from breaking that law. He'd obviously not done a good enough job frightening her on her last late night walk through here. He'd need to do better this time.

"Max?"

He bounded out onto the path, raised his hackles and growled at her. He would not be above giving her comfort later in the form of naked snuggling to help her get over the fright of being hunted by a big wolf. Scaring her was a horrible thing to do when she was already worried about something else, but she absolutely had to learn this lesson.

Gal jumped back a foot and put her hand over her heart. Good. Max put the darkest menace into his growl as he could. His wolf was rolling its eyes at him. She was no prey or threat, it would prefer to go lick her from head to toe and back again. His beast liked her. A lot. Maybe because of the way she seemed to sparkle in the moonlight.

No. Bad wolf. Bad, bad wolf.

Max howled just for good measure. Both Gal and his wolf needed to know who was in charge here.

"Thank heavens." Gal rushed forward and threw her arms around his neck and buried her face in the warmth of his fur.

She hugged him so tight he didn't know what else to do, so he plopped down on his haunches, waiting for her to release him. Gal sniffled for another moment into his scruff and then sat back. She grabbed his face between her hands and looked deep into his eyes. "I need to get a message to Max. Please."

Max whimpered, louder than he meant to. It was either that or speak into her mind again and that was a very bad idea. He was doing an awful job at scaring her away. That was a losing battle. His wolf laughed at him and licked her cheek where a tear had streaked down.

That got him a smile. Damn, she was beautiful. And in danger if he didn't get her out of these woods to find out what had her scared and searching for him in the first place.

He had an idea, but it was risky. Gal was smart and she probably wasn't far from figuring out who and what he was anyway. This is why wolves didn't date humans. She was intelligent, but it was a real stretch to think he and the wolf were one and the same. It would probably be better if he could steer her toward thinking the wolf was some sort of pet.

There went his wolf rolling its eyes again. Whatever. It was the best idea he had.

Max wiggled away, pretended like he heard something in the woods, looked from Gal to the woods again and then ran off. Moon above he hoped she understood his message from those less than stellar acting skills. She hadn't followed so he ran as fast as he could back to the clearing to get his clothes.

He shifted and shoved his legs into the pants and shoes and took off back toward the path. He couldn't run in human form even half as fast as his wolf, especially while trying to put a shirt over his head and not crashing into a tree because he'd put his arm through the head hole and his head through the arm and couldn't see.

A hundred yards away he put his plan, that was feeling more and more lame by the moment, into action. Max whistled and then called out, "Wolfie? Come here boy."

"Max? Max! Over here." Gal jumped up and down, waving her hands, and then ran toward him. "Max. Thank goodness I found you. I knew you had a connection to that wolf."

He pretended to ignore that last part of her sentence and focus on the rest. "What did you need to find me for? What's wrong, *lapochka*?"

Gal looked over and around his shoulder, back into the woods where he'd come from, and rubbed her arms. "We went to the sheriff's department."

The blood in Max's arteries and veins went sub-zero. He had to grit his teeth to hide the outward chill shaking up his spine. "The sheriff's?"

If those fuckers touched a hair on her head, arm, leg, or even her big toe, he was going to eat them all for breakfast. His wolf pushed hard to get back out, make sure the area was secure, protect her at all costs.

She nodded her head and bit her bottom lip. "But they didn't believe us. The sheriff wasn't even there, just some stupid lackeys who told us they couldn't do anything until she's missing for twenty-four hours. Max, she could be dead. All the TV shows say the first few hours are critical to finding a missing person."

Wait, what? He should have fucking warned her the Sheriff's department was....what? The bad kind of werewolves? Yeah, no. He could have at least said they were corrupt and not to try to contact anyone but him if there was more trouble.

"Gal, babe, slow down a second and catch me up. Who is missing, what were you reporting to the sheriff's?" Dammit. He'd been close enough to her for the other two incidents that she hadn't had a chance to call 9-1-1. The first was dumb luck. He should have known better after that. He'd have to schedule enforcers to keep an eye on the girls from here on out if he couldn't be there himself. His father hadn't questioned yet why these women in particular were being targeted, and he wouldn't be able to for several days. Max could deal with this.

She had to blink back tears and her voice wavered. "Zara. She's gone. I think she's been taken. You have to believe me. She wouldn't just leave and not say anything. Not after last night."

Max's stomach dropped like a hot rock. If Niko weren't already dead, he'd kill Max for letting his girl get kidnapped by the Grimms. Because there was no doubt in his mind that's what had happened. Retaliation for killing the sheriff and taking Key.

Doc had that poor girl under close observation. She kept rambling on about dragons and witches and wolves at a bar. Her mind was either broken by whatever those bastards had done to her or she was having prophetic visions. For her sake, he hoped it was the former because at least she could heal from that. It seemed unlikely if she was a psychic prophet no one would have known. But if she was, that would be an obvious reason for the Grimms to have taken her.

"I think I know who has her."

So why had they taken Zara? Whatever the reason he had to act fast to get her back, and that meant doing something with some serious consequences. If his pack found out, they may never trust him again. Hard to be the alpha and enforce wolf law if he'd broken it himself.

Even harder to be a leader who couldn't make the tough decisions. Saving a woman's life, especially one who was important to a member of the pack, dead or alive, had to be more important than preserving their secret. He had to trust that Gal wouldn't freak out, that he could trust her, that the entire Troika pack could trust her.

"I was worried you might. Max, what's going on with you, your family? Am I going to have to go into the Witness Protection program?" There wasn't the slightest hint of joking in her voice.

"No, you won't. Gal, we aren't in the mafia. Although it would probably be safer to let you think we were."

"What's worse than the dark underworld of organized crime? Oh, man. Zara's already dead isn't she? She's hanging in a meat locker somewhere. Are Heli and I next? Shouldn't we call the FBI? I'm sure they'd make you a deal."

Uh-oh. Fear was pouring off of her in waves of words and the scent of spoiled fruit. She was on the verge of freaking out which meant it was now or never. Either she continued to freak and he'd have to take her to Doc to sit in the nice padded room with Key, or she'd understand that he and his family would protect her for the rest of her life.

Galyna was about to become a Troika, whether she wanted to or not.

God forgive him.

"Shh, shh, shh." He pulled her into his arms and held her tight. He needed the strength from her as much as he needed his own wolf's strength. "*Lapochka*, I'm going to let you in on a secret. I don't want you to freak out, although you might a little bit anyway. But more importantly, you can never tell anyone. Not your family, not your friends. No one."

"Okay. Lay it on me." She stepped back and made the signal with her hands to bring it on. "Although, you should know, I've already planned my WitSec cover story. What do you think of the name Jane? It's nice and boring. No one will come looking for a Jane, who works at the grocery store, and runs a book club on Thursday nights, right?"

"I promise. No WitSec. I'm trusting you to keep my secret. Trust me that I will protect you. Okay?"

Gal's throat bobbed as she swallowed. She didn't want this, and it was probably going to ruin any chance he had at a relationship with her. He'd never been so nervous in his entire life. Not the first time he shifted, not the first time he'd kissed a girl, not ever.

The muscles in his chest contracted and he swallowed hard. Now or never.

Max raised his face to the waxing moon and slowly let the shift take over his body. His bones cracked and bent, reshaping themselves into their supernatural form. His skin split and burst allowing his new shape to take over and his fur to protect him. His teeth elongated and became sharp and deadly.

The clothes he wore fell to the ground in a shredded heap and Max stood in the center of them on four paws and silently waited for Gal's reaction.

I KNEW IT!

*T*ingles rushed all up and down and across and
sideways and inside out of Gal's skin. Not the bad
kind that signaled her flight or flight response was kicking in.
Nope. This feeling was more like sugar cubes were melting in
her heart.

The wolf.

Max was the grey wolf.

Unbelievable. Yet not. It all made perfect sense. The signs
had all been there. The universe was practically screaming at
her to figure it out.

The wolf that was Max sat down on his haunches and
made the sweetest little whine. Oh, geez. He was waiting for
her to say something. She'd barely even reacted. She'd simply
stared at him, with her jaw hanging open wide enough for the
flies to get in. He was probably freaking out. Should she pet
him on the head? She had the urge to thrust one hand up in
the air, Superman style and whisper shout 'Yes!' to the forest.
But Max had said she needed to keep this a secret.

In the end, she went with a little clap and a whispered

"yay." Which she was rather proud of herself for. Especially since inside she was clapping up a storm, cheerleader pom-pom style. A teeny tiny part of her said she should be freaked out. The rest told that part to quit being a grumpy-grump baby and see this for what it was.

Really. Effing. Cool.

The wolf turned its head sideways like a funny puppy trying to figure her weirdness out. Maybe he couldn't understand English in his wolf form. "Max? Can you understand me?"

Yes, lapochka.

"Whoa. You're psychic too?" Gal pressed her fingers to her head and closed her eyes tight. "What am I thinking now?"

I can't read your mind. I'm a little surprised you can even hear me. Mindspeak is a connection that is usually only for our kind and others like us.

He couldn't seriously be telling her monsters were real. Ooh. Maybe unicorns were too. Gasp. And mermaids. No. No. That was silly. She was being ridiculous. He probably meant other werewolf type things. Like rugaroos, maybe Bigfoot, and chupacabras. At least those had a basis in crypto-zoology which she had guided many a young reader toward in the 001s and the 398s. But you know what else old Dewey had put in the 398 section? Fairy tales. "What do you mean others?"

Dragons, other animals shifters like bears, lions, foxes, you know.

"Okay, okay. I can buy that there might be other shifter animals, but dragons? Come on. You're kidding." Please don't be kidding.

Dragons are real. Real assholes if you ask me. The whole lot of them are so totally focused on fighting off the demon dragon plague that they put it above all else. They don't know how to even have a little fun.

She blinked trying to process more new information. Anymore blowing of her mind and she was going to run out of brain cells. "A demon plague? Humans can't catch it can they?"

It would explain why creepy Mr. Sinul who used the library computers to look at porn always seemed to have a new boil on his face. Definitely the demon plague.

Max made a huffing sound that she thought might be a wolf laugh. *No. Demon dragons are not a disease, they are beasts from hell. They haven't been seen in the Americas for centuries, so you have no need to worry about them. There is a lot for you to learn about my world, Galyna. I will answer all your questions in time.*

He stood up and kicked his shredded clothing into the underbrush. *For now though, I need you to swear to me you will keep this secret. It is forbidden for wolves to show their true selves to humans. I've broken wolf law because I trust you. We both must be prepared for the consequences.*

A lump formed in her throat. She wasn't sure if it was because of those mentioned consequences or because Max trusted her with something so important. Gal raised her right hand in the air. "I swear on my soul, that you can trust me. I will tell no one what I've seen."

Thank you. I'd love to sit with you and show you the forest and let you scratch my ears, but I've shared this with you because I couldn't see any other alternative. We're going to have to work together. I'm afraid Zara had been taken by a rival pack and she is in danger.

The pack. Duh. That explained everything else. The Troikas weren't mafia, they were a pack. Packs had alphas. Gal bet Selena fulfilled that roll. "Wait, is your mom a wolf too?"

Of course. Where do you think my brothers and I came from?

Aha. Kosta and Niko were wolf-shifters too. That explained so much. But not how they had all come to be... she couldn't call them monsters, they weren't. How they had all become supernatural beings. "A werewolf bit you?"

Some of the legends of werewolves do come from our past, but that's not exactly how it works. There is a mate's bite, but it's not...

Mates. Another piece of the puzzle fell into place. The creepy home intruders had called her and the sisters little mates. Apparently that wasn't Australian. What was he going to say about mate's and biting. Oh man, had those men wanted to bite her and the sisters, make them be their wolf mates? "Not what?"

We need to go. There are other wolves in the Reserve. Follow me and try to move as quietly as you can.

Gal expected him to turn back into a human and then realized his clothes were in a heap under a bush. They weren't wearable. Which meant if he shifted, he'd be naked.

Naked.

Gal fanned herself and then hurried to catch up to Max. He took her off the regular walking path and into the forest. She laughed at herself for thinking of the scene in Little Red Riding Hood where the wolf leads the little girl away with all the pretty flowers. Except, Gal kind of hoped that Max would eat her up.

She followed the wolf through the woods, then through a couple of neighborhoods until they ended up all the way down by the beach. If she was going to be dating a wolf shifter, maybe she should start working out. This was way more exercise than she was used to getting and her muscles and feet were screaming at her. She didn't let Max know. If he was taking her to wherever he thought Zara was being held, she would suffer through the pain. Thus far it wasn't anything a good long hot bath couldn't fix.

She'd bear any pain if it meant rescuing her friend.

Max led her all the way to the edge of town where Rogue intersected with Bay City. The Bay County Sheriff's department wasn't far. "Why are you taking me back to the sheriff? Those dickheads didn't do anything when I came crying to them earlier."

We need to see if Zara is here. Max sniffed the air. *I haven't caught her scent, but they could be masking it.*

Hold up. "You think the sheriff is working with your rival pack? Why would they do that? I thought wolves weren't supposed to reveal themselves to humans. Wait, is it blackmail of some kind? Do they have dirt on the sheriff? I never trusted that guy."

Love, I don't think they are working with anyone. The sheriff's department is mostly staffed with wolves from the Grimm pack, including the sheriff. Who is dead. Until recently, they were our allies. Now they are... not.

Wow. The Troikas might not be mafia, but this whole wolf pack thing was not far from it. The Cosa Moonstra. "Crap. Then we have to go in there, like right now. I made a huge stink about telling the whole world that they wouldn't help me, and they'd be hearing from my lawyers etcetera. They're going to know I went to you. I just know they are. What if they hurt her? I promised Heli I would find her."

Don't freak out yet. My wolves have been making their way

here for the last hour and we have the place surrounded. The Grimms inside are cut off from their alpha and they won't make a move without his say so. But with you, we have the element of surprise. Trust me, no one is going to think that I revealed the pack to you.

"Me? I don't know what you think I'm going to do. Read them a story with finger puppets? Catalog all their records in the Dewey Decimal system? Shush them?" Max being a wolf was badass. Her being a librarian wasn't useful at all. She didn't really even understand why he'd brought her along or even let her in on his big bad wolf secret.

Sure, she liked him a lot, and she was really happy he trusted her enough that he could show her this part of himself. But she couldn't exactly do anything about it. Gal shook her head. "I've already put Zara in deeper trouble by opening my mouth. She wouldn't even be here if it wasn't for me. I don't think I can help."

Max had been standing next to her, but he shoved her with his nose so that she had to back up to a wall. Geez, he and his nose were strong.

That's not true. This is not your fault. It's my family's and we will get you girls out of this.

His eyes glowed a brilliant blue around the edges and his fur seemed to sparkle. His wolf form was absolutely stunning and it had her heart skipping a beat. He pressed up against her and gave her a big slobbery lick to the face.

"Ugh. Max. Gross." That was not how she liked getting kisses from him.

It pulled you out of that freak-out spiral, didn't it? If not, I will happily lick you again. Somewhere else.

"Don't be gross. But you're right. That helped. I'm gonna

keep freaking out a little bit. But I'll do whatever I can to help Zara."

Good. Let's -- Max turned his head and his ears pricked up. Another wolf, a big black one came right into their hiding spot. While Max's eyes were a brilliant blue, this wolf's were similar but with a definite purple undertone to them. Max snorted at him and they looked at each other, heads tilting and bobbing, and their tails swished.

Interesting. Wolf body language. She realized they must be talking to each other in their minds. "Hey, you two want to let me in on the conversation? Also, who are you?"

The black wolf barked at her and then its body contorted and grew until a six-foot two, butt-naked, Kosta stood in front of her. "You shouldn't be here, Galyna."

"Whoa, buddy. I do not want to see your junk." Gal slapped one hand over her eyes and the other she held out covering Kosta's ample baby-maker. Okay, so yeah. She'd caught a peek. If Max was even half so well endowed she wouldn't be disappointed. "Geez. I am so putting together an in-case-of-emergency-shifting kits so that every time you guys turn back into humans I don't have to see anyone's, uh, manhoods."

"Galyna." Max's human voice had her jumping about a foot.

She hadn't expected him to shift too and now all she wanted was to yank her hand from her eyes and see what he had below the belt. She was so going to hell for thinking about sex at a time like this. "Can we please find Zara and go."

"Max told me your theory, but she's not here. The enforcers have the building surrounded and there is no sign of her."

Gal opened her fingers enough to see Max and Kosta's

faces. "You're a thousand percent sure Zara isn't here? What if they're, you know, masking her scent, or have her locked up in a sub basement or something."

"Not a chance. This nose would know. Is Heli alright?" Kosta folded his arms and stroked his beard with one hand. He was worried. Maybe his relationship with Heli was more than the fling she thought it was.

"Yeah, she went over to her parent's house to see if they'd heard from Zara. She's going to stay the rest of the night there just in case. She's pretty panicked." If Zara wasn't being kept by the bad guy wolves at the sheriff's department where else could she be? Max was going to have a lot more explaining to do about this pack war thing. If there was one thing Gal knew how to do it was pull lots of moving pieces of a project together and find the answers. That masters degree had to come in useful for something more than her $28,000 a year job.

Although, she hadn't figured it out with the whole Max is a werewolf thing. No, she couldn't think that way. It was a lot to ask someone to suspend their beliefs to come to a conclusion like that. If Max and Kosta, and whoever else knew anything, would give her all the pieces of the puzzle she knew she could work out how to find Zara. She just needed more information.

Kosta nodded and pointed at Max. "You owe me a beer and a burger and a long discussion about what the hell you were thinking, big brother. Tomorrow, or at least sometime before dad gets back and he and mom kill you."

Eek. She coughed, trying to get her breath back. "Kill you?"

Max had mentioned that revealing this secret to her had consequences. But the death penalty? That seemed harsh.

Especially if she never told anyone. Which she wouldn't. That certainly put a damper on him telling her anything else. Without a lot more information she wouldn't be able to help Zara. Crapolla. She would have to find a way to prove to Kosta, and probably the rest of the pack, that she could be trusted.

"We'll see about that." Max clasped Kosta's shoulder, and Kosta returned the embrace. "Go. Check on Heli, see if you can find anything else out about Zara's disappearance. I'll take care of the rest of the enforcers."

Kosta shifted back into the black wolf and took off back toward Rogue's residential area. Gal shivered. That sound their bones and whatever else inside their bodies made when they changed from human to wolf sounded painful and horrible. She wasn't sure how she was going to get used to that.

They watched Kosta run off and Max waited until his brother was out of sight before he said anything more. "If Zara isn't here, that changes my plans. Give me a minute to give the enforcers new assignments and then I'll take you home. Stay hidden. Okay?"

Gal nodded and slunk against the wall, her hand still mostly covering her eyes. She would never admit it to Max, but she peeked. She couldn't help it. Max had already turned away and all she caught was a glimpse of his butt. What a butt it was.

If she hadn't been thinking about Max's derriere she might not have seen the pair of glowing eyes, looking right at her from behind a tree. She tried to swallow and call for Max but fear had stuck a giant boulder in her throat and nothing but a teeny croak came out. That croak turned into a squeak when a second, a third, and a fourth set of eyes blinked on like Christmas lights all in a row.

The first set of eyes moved closer and Gal pressed herself tighter against the wall. Think. Think. She had a brain, she needed to use it. She'd had encounters with several wolves now, and the bad guys had all had a glow around their irises in shades of red and orange. Max and Kosta's had been shades of blue. What color were the eyes coming toward her now? She squinted, praying for blue.

Yes, they were. Phew. Hopefully that meant these wolves were on Team Troika. Only one way to find out. "Hello, I'm Galyna. I'm here with Max. Please don't bite me."

The wolf in the lead did that snuffling sound she'd associated with a laugh when Max had done it. He trotted up close and wasn't growling, so she might have a chance at not dying.

"What's going on, guys? Max just went to--" Uh-oh. He'd gone to talk to these guys. If they were here and not over by the sheriff's office, either Max was in trouble, or she was.

The wolf in the front of the small group did the weird contortionist thing and shifted. One by one, the wolves behind him did the same until a wall of muscle and peen was standing in front of her in a semi-circle. So many penises.

None the one she wanted.

Covering her eyes hadn't done a bit of good last time, so Gal simply kept her eyes up. "What can I do for you, penises, I mean gentleman?"

The men glanced around at each other and gave the guy who'd led them all over here some kind of go ahead. "You're the woman Maxsim Troika is in love with."

The night air went from cool to hot and humid. Or maybe that was only her.

Love? "I don't know about in love with, but we're umm, exploring a relationship. We trust each other if that's what you're asking."

The wolf chuckled. "Not asking. We all know it, even if you do not yet. It's hard to hide base feelings from another wolf. We can smell fear, desire, hate, love, and so much more."

Murmurs of assent went through the group. This wasn't awkward at all. Half the pack knew Max was in love with her but she didn't. If they could smell desire it meant Max had known exactly how turned on she was by him all the time.

That didn't mean they were in love. Sure, she liked him a lot, and she definitely wanted to see him naked instead of all of his friends. But love? No. This was more like lust. Wasn't it? "Okay, so you're what, the Valentine's Day committee? If there's going to be singing and a candy-gram, I'm going to have to insist you put some clothes on."

Another guy stepped forward. This one she recognized. He was one of the bartenders at Sleepy Folk. Harley. That was his name. "No singing. We want you to give a message to Maxsim."

"Me? Why can't you tell him. You work with him and you're in his pack. Right?" She hadn't actually cleared that up. This whole conversation could be a ruse to distract her, get her to let her guard down so they could kidnap her too. She tried to move away, but her back was already up against the wall of the building. Her heart thumped hard against her chest and she looked around for an escape route. Where the hell was Max?

"Yes, we are." Harley said. "We're loyal to the Troika pack and we will always protect those our alpha's heir hold dear. You don't have any reason to fear us, *malish*. What we didn't know for sure until tonight was whether Max was one of us. Now that he has revealed our truth to you, we know he is on our side."

"Your side? What side is that? Your pack politics are new and still confusing to me." If packs had coalitions within she was going to need to make a chart to keep them all straight.

"It's very simple. We are all in love with human women too. We want to take them as our mates, but it is forbidden for wolves to mate with humans."

Oh. Ohhhhh. "Is mating like marriage?"

"Only in that the pair promises themselves to the other, but the mating alliance is much more than that. Humans pretend their vows are for life, but when a wolf mates, it truly is until death. The bond is unbreakable."

The warmth of the night had somehow wormed its way into her chest and was spreading for her core outward. Her skin tingled with the heat. "Okay. What can I do about it. Do you need wolf divorces? I'm not a lawyer, I'm a librarian."

"We want Max to lift the ban on telling humans who and what we are and allow us to mate who we want."

"Is he in a position to do that?"

"He is the alpha's heir. If he mates you, the rest of us can have that freedom too."

*M*ax asked a few of the enforcers to keep an eye on Gal while he bolted back to the Reserve and grabbed his car where he always kept a spare set of clothes. She'd been hyped up on adrenaline, fear, and excitement when he came across her in the woods, but they'd burned through most of that as he pushed her to hike to hell and gone.

One would think out of any person in the entire world he would realize she was human. The human with limitations. A human he could never have, and the one he wasn't sure he could live without. A human who was not a wolf.

Revealing his true self to her created a bond that he couldn't allow to ever be broken. One that could destroy both of them. Because he had no idea how to keep her a secret. But he did know one person who knew how to work the system better than anyone else in the world.

His mother.

She was either going to kill him softly, like with poisoned cookies and a song, or help him. She did make really good murder cookies. He'd never see it coming. He crossed his fingers she would understand and the situation wouldn't come to that.

He rolled into the parking lot of the strip mall in Bay City that was adjacent to the sheriff's department. He didn't want to tip them off so blatantly that he was nearby and watching them. His old Impala wasn't the quietest of get away cars. He parked, trotted over to where he'd left Gal hiding. She still had that faint sparkle to her skin, but he found her looking even more exhausted than when he'd left.

Shit. She was his responsibility and he'd done a crappy-ass job of protecting her so far. "Come on, *lapochka*. Let me take you home."

She rubbed her arms and a little vee formed between her eyebrows. "What about Zara?"

"I've got the pack sitting on this place. Any move they make, we'll know about it. We aren't going to do her any good sitting out here falling asleep. We'll go home, get some rest, and start fresh again in the morning."

She shifted from foot to foot and glanced back at the brick building the enforcers had surrounded. She opened her mouth like she was going to say something and then shut it again.

"What is it?"

"Nothing. Let's go."

Max waited one more moment before he moved to lead her across to the car. There was definitely something she wanted to say to him, but was either afraid or didn't know how.

Which stank. Not literally. He didn't scent real fear on her, only reticence.

He'd showed her his deepest darkest secret and she was worried about talking to him. Did she not trust him? That didn't feel right. She did trust him. She trusted him enough that she'd followed a wolf through the forest and straight to human law enforcement. She could have freaking called animal control on him. She could have run from him the second he shifted.

She hadn't done either of those things. She'd clapped and whispered the quietest cheer of happiness.

His heart had soared and he'd felt a huge weight lifted. He'd never felt so light in his life.

So, what had happened in the seven minutes he'd been gone? He caught the scent of other wolves around her, but only ones that were supposed to be here. His pack, his men. No way they had scared her into silence. He made sure to ask the enforcers he knew had human women in their lives to take point. They all had an unsaid understanding. That couldn't be the problem.

Maybe she was changing her mind about him. Moon above he was being a dumbass, analyzing the shit out of one simple action. Whatever was on her mind, she would tell him eventually. Or she wouldn't and he'd get it out of her with his own brand of torture. Which involved kisses and tickling. "Come on, I grabbed my car. I'll drive you home."

Gal blinked, surprised. "You did? Well, good. I'm not going to say no to a ride. My feet are killing me."

He grabbed her hand and led her to the car. "Maybe I'll give you a foot rub later."

"Something else I wouldn't say no to. Make it a full on massage and I might just give you my undying love." Gal laughed already more relaxed and got into the car.

Max froze, staring at the black shiny rooftop. It had been a joke. She hadn't meant it.

Her undying love.

Every fiber of his being from wolf to man wanted that more than anything in the world. More than making his parents proud by being alpha, more than fighting off the threat from the Grimms, more than he wanted his next breath. He wanted Gal to love him.

Because he loved her.

He was so fucked.

Max blew out a long breath, shook his head at himself and climbed into the car. The cab was already filled with the scent of her, and it went straight from his nose to his cock. The natural scent of her was the greatest aphrodisiac and he was going to have to be very careful not to react. He couldn't control the way his pants got tight, sitting here next to her, but he could hold back the groan pushing at the back of his throat, and his wolf inside growling to get out and claim what was his.

He cleared his throat. "Okay, so home?"

"I kind of don't want to go back there and be all by myself."

Shit, shit, shit. She was asking him to stay over. There was no way he could control himself if he did that. No, sleeping at her house, whether he was in her bed, her room, or even under the same roof without a chaperone was a very bad idea. Where else could he take her?

Max turned the key and gave the car a little rev to get her going as fast as possible. He tore out of the parking lot and headed toward the one place he would not be able to give in to this all encompassing need to kiss her, bite her, fuck her.

His mother's house.

Besides. His mom would be much less likely to end him with Gal standing right there.

It took only a few minutes for Gal to figure out where they were headed. "Oh. I don't want to impose on your mother. She must need--"

She stopped mid sentence and turned sideways on the long bench seat to face him. "All those packs of clothes and things I saw at your mom's house, they're for when everyone shifts and needs new clothes, aren't they? But where were all the men's clothes? Do little kids shift too? Do all pack members keep stashes like that at their houses? How many pack members are there?"

The questions might keep pouring out of her if he didn't give her some answers pretty quick. It was more than cute how inquisitive she was. He really liked how her brain worked on high speed all the time. "Whoa, whoa, Gal. One at a time."

She clamped her mouth shut, folded her hands in her lap, and looked at him expectantly. See. Adorable.

"My parents' home, the whole estate is the pack headquarters. Any Troika pack member is welcome there anytime, so we have a steady stream coming and going. My mother keeps extra clothes not just for shifting, but in case of emergencies when we might need to call the women and children in to one safe location that we can defend."

"Like during a pack war?"

The lightness from earlier was rapidly fading. "Yes. This started off more like a dispute, but the situation is quickly devolving and with no Tzar to bring down an iron fist, I'm afraid our little pack battle is going to become an all out all pack war."

"Tzar? Like in Russia? Were the Romanoff's wolf shifters?"

Max chuckled. "No. They weren't, but long before their reign a wolf shifter did sit on the throne. During the dark ages my people were unruly and humans rightly feared us. We were hunted almost to extinction. The first of the Volkov's took the throne and changed everything. The packs all swore an oath to disappear from human society and keep our kind a secret. Those that didn't were killed."

"But you clearly live among the rest of us now."

"After a few hundred years our numbers recovered and it was difficult to keep our packs hidden. When humans began crossing the ocean and settling in America, we came along pretending to be any other immigrants. With our success integrating into society, but still keeping our true selves a secret, the Tzar slowly allowed the packs in Russia and Europe to do the same."

"You said there is no Tzar now. What happened? What instigated this war?"

"The Tzar," Max sighed, "was assassinated about a month ago, and he had no heir. Packs around the world are using that as an excuse to run amok. There are many who don't agree that we should remain hidden."

"Do you think you should?"

No one had ever asked him that before. In fact, he'd never had an in depth discussion about pack politics with anyone before. You either believed what the alpha believed or you were the bad guy. He really hadn't worked out what his own feelings were. "It's not that simple. Those who want the end of that law, they call themselves one-bloods. They don't want to just come out and tell humans we exist. They believe shifters are superior to humans and we should rule over them."

"Geez. They sound like white supremacists, like Nazis. Do you think everyone who wants to end the secrecy feel that way, or are there other groups who simply aren't voicing their opinions fearing backlash from the one-bloods?"

"I don't know. I think you're probably right. There may even be some in my own pack who'd like to reveal themselves to select special humans in their lives."

"Huh. I, uh, bet there are."

Max pulled into the driveway of his mother's house and switched off the car. He could happily sit here talking to Gal like this for hours. His family and most of his pack probably wouldn't think revealing his true nature to her was a good decision, but he would never think otherwise. This one short but deep conversation with her had solidified ideas in his own mind about how all of wolf kind operated and how he might become a better leader to his own pack someday.

She would make a good wolf matriarch. He'd already broken one law, would another make much of a difference?

They walked into the house, hand in hand, and where he had planned to separate himself from her touch when they found his mother, he decided not to. "Mom. Galyna's back with us for another night. There have been developments in the skirmish with the Grimms. They've taken Zara."

To her credit, Selena didn't even blink twice when Max spoke about pack politics in front of Gal. She simply nodded and got up to make drinks for them all. "If it's just us tonight, I'll get one of the guest rooms ready. You can tell me more about what our plans are to recover your brother's mate over dinner."

Max nodded and then what his mother said hit him over the head like a ton of lead-filled bricks. He literally lost his footing and had to grab onto Gal's hand a little tighter to remain upright. "Mom?"

"Oh don't be so dramatic, *sinochek*. It's not like we didn't all know he was head over heels in love with her. It's perfectly obvious she's the perfect match for him. It would be a great dishonor to his memory if we pretended anything otherwise."

"Wait. His memory?" Gal touched his arm. "Max, where is Niko? Zara thinks he's in Russia."

Fuck a duck. "He is. He was. Damn. Remember, I said the Tzar was assassinated and that started this whole war?"

Gal went all wide eyed and looked between him and his mother. "Holy crap. Niko was the Tzar?"

"No, *kroshka*," Selena interjected saving him from having to admit such a dark failing to her himself. "Nikolaus is accused of killing Tzar Mikhail Volkov. I refuse to believe it. They say he is dead, killed by the Tzar's guard while trying to escape. So, we mourn his death."

Gal stared hard at Max's mother, who stared hard back. "You don't believe he's dead, do you?"

Max was finding it hard to swallow at that moment.

Selena shrugged. "Some things a mother knows. Some things she does not. I simply have a feeling that the Troika brothers' story is not finished."

He should have spent more time with his mother this past month. They'd gone from Niko's death to war so fast that they didn't have time to grieve. She was in the denial stage. Max understood. He certainly hadn't made peace with any of the changes and his mother hated change. "Mom, we all wish Niko wasn't gone."

She waved him off, but not before he caught a glimpse of her wolf shining behind her eyes. "Enough. There is nothing more to discuss right now. Except what kind of wine you'd like with dinner and how we will take over the Grimm pack and crush their balls under our claws."

Selena walked off into the kitchen and he and Gal quietly watched her go. Gal leaned closer and whispered, "your mom is kinda fucking cool."

"I know." Didn't mean he wasn't a little worried about her. But giving her a project. He could see she was already scheming something that had to do with him bringing Galyna home.

The three of them ate dinner together and discussed more ins and outs of pack politics, the implications of one-bloods infiltrating nearby packs, and how to find Zara. Selena answered all of Gal's questions, and didn't seemed fazed in the least that she was laying out hundreds of years of wolf-shifter secrets to a human. She treated Gal like she was already part of the pack.

Max was good with all of it until Gal asked about mates.

"Zara and Niko weren't married. She doesn't even know he's a wolf, does she? How can she be his mate?"

Selena sat back and took a sip of wine. She looked at Max, then over to Gal, and back with a grin on her face. Uh-oh. Max knew that look. It was never good. His mother had machinations with him in mind. "Since the beginning of the reign of the Volkov's, wolf shifters have mated wolf-shifters. We could not intermingle with humans, so there was no other choice. We learned as a species to suppress our need to find our fated mate."

"Fated mates are a fairy tale." He didn't believe in happy ever-afters. Did he?

"No. They are not." His mother rolled her eyes at him.

Never a good sign. "Every shifter has a true mate, the one that the fates have chosen especially for them. It comes with the magic that gives us the ability to be two forms in one. Two must always become one. A few of our kind still find their way to their true mate, but many do not simply because we were forbidden to look."

"The only thing forbidden is to reveal ourselves to humans." That and to bite them. Which suddenly seemed like a strange taboo to Max. A wolf's bite didn't turn a human into a shifter like in the movies. But the sheriff had clearly bitten Key, and it had changed her.

"Exactly." His mom raised an eyebrow and her wine glass toasting his statement.

Okay, he could buy that humans might be true mates to wolves. He sure as hell felt something more than simple lust when it came to Galyna. But how would he know? It had to be more than a feeling. It had to. "If that was true how would anyone even know if they'd met their true mate?"

"Finding a true mate may be hampered, but the old traditions haven't changed in a millennium, Maxsim." She was telling him in so many words he was being a dumbass and the answer was right in front of him.

"The mating ceremony? It's just a ritual." He'd witnessed dozens of them and there had never been anything special. Nothing more than the wolf equivalent to a wedding. But without the flouncy dresses and a lot more biting and sex.

"For most. But for a lucky few, it's when they know they've found their true mate. The full moon is only a few nights away. You'll see." She did that thing where she looked between the two of them all meaningful-like. Did she really think Gal might be his true mate? It wasn't like she was going to be allowed at the mating ritual with a dozen packs there and his father bringing some wolftress for him. He'd be expected to forge alliances, not whimper about true love.

"Dad is your true mate? Is that how you know about all of this?" Maybe if his parents had been lucky enough to find a true mate, he could too. Maybe his father would understand if Gal turned out to be his fated mate.

"He isn't. But we have made a strong alpha pair and we got you three out of the deal. So it all worked out. But who is to say what would have happened if I'd made a different choice and followed the fate laid out for me by wolf law." Selena pressed her lips together and gave him and Gal a sad smile. She got up from the table, took her wine glass, and went into the kitchen.

"Holy crow. Dude." Gal grabbed his hand. "Your mom knows who her true mate is and it's not your dad."

Max had a feeling his mother knew exactly who his true mate was too. It wasn't any wolftress from another pack his father was bringing home either.

He'd already revealed his true form to a human and his mother hadn't even blinked twice. Instead she told him a fairy tale and given him a sad warning about choices. She was crafty, his mother. A smart son always did what his mother told him to do.

Max may not be as big and strong as Niko, but he was smart.

Tonight he was going to prove that. He stood up from the table and held his hand out to Gal. She took it with a smile. Max kissed her knuckles and pulled her up and into his arms. "Come on, *kiska*. There's something I've been wanting to do with you since the first second I knew you were back in town."

Actually, it was something he'd wanted since they were in school, but until tonight he never could have admitted even to himself that he'd been in love with Galyna his whole life.

Max led Galyna down a hall she hadn't seen the last time she was here. This was going toward a part of the house that seemed more on the private side. There were family pictures on the walls instead of art and she caught a peek into bedrooms that had at some point definitely belonged to teenage boys.

"Wait. Is this your old room?" She tried to stick her head into a room with blue walls and a poster of an old muscle car that looked a lot like Max's hung slightly askew on the wall.

He yanked her away. "It is, and tomorrow I'll let you gawk at my teenage awkwardness all you want."

Gal laughed right at him. "You were never weird like the rest of us. Did you even see the size of my glasses back then? No, you were the popular hot guy they make teen heart throb movies about."

Max guided her into the last doorway at the end of the hall and into a sumptuous bedroom with a huge bigger than king-sized bed, and a bevy of romantic candles lit and scattered throughout the space. The scene took her breath away. It was perfectly romantic.

He pulled her into his arms and rubbed his cheek against hers. "I was awkward around you."

If this was how wolf-men started the foreplay, she liked it. Gal tipped her head to the other side so he could rub her other cheek. "Me? When did you even say more than three words to me before the other night?"

He nuzzled her starting at her jaw and worked his way down her neck and back to her ear. "I didn't, because every time I tried my brain froze up and my dick got hard and I'd have to hide in the bathroom thinking of baseball and England or whatever had nothing to do with the way your ass swayed from side to side as you walked toward class."

Oh man. The way his breath wisped across her skin had her eyes rolling back in her head, it felt so good, and naughty at the same time. It was almost enough to distract her from his completely made up story about having a crush on her in school. "No way. You... no. I am not going to believe for a second that you had a crush on me in high school. Max, I would have died and thought I'd gone to good-girl heaven if you'd even--"

He cut off all her denials by pushing his hands into her hair, pulling her head back, and crushing his mouth down on hers. He pushed his way into her mouth testing and teasing her, forcing her mind to give up its protests in favor of some- thing much more fun. She couldn't get enough of him, of the way he was devouring her with the intensity of his kisses. He went from foreplay to full-on need in an instant taking her with him.

Gal ran her fingers under his shirt and backed up toward

the big bed pulling him with her. They bumped into it and she sat, breaking their kiss. "That thing you've been wanting to do with me... it had better be to take me to bed. But I'm warning you Max, if your phone rings this time, I'm shoving it up your butt and not in a fun way."

"Wow, *kiska*, your dirty talk is turning me on." He pushed her back onto the mattress and crawled up over her. "Say something else naughty."

"Be careful what you wish for, you scallywag." She was barely keeping a nervous giggle in. He was clearly a sex god and she was nothing more than the librarian who cata- logued books about sex and gods. But boy did she have an encyclopedic knowledge of both. It had to come in handy eventually. Now or never, nerdy girl. She might be horrible at talking dirty, but he wasn't. She'd just have to get him to give up on even attempting to get her to do it and take over. "I'm a librarian and happen to know a litany of medieval and Shakespearean swear words that will knock your socks off."

Max drew her arms up over her head and captured them in one hand. "Seeing as we're both fully clothed, I think my socks and yours need knocking off."

Okay, Shakespeare hadn't done it. Time to bring out the big guns. "Just remember you asked for it. Come on down here and sard me, you rapscallion. Sard me so hard, you turn me into a driggle-draggle."

His eyes twinkled and his lips moved into a mischievous grin. "Good try, my dirty librarian. How about instead I strip you naked so I can finally lick, and kiss, and touch, and caress every inch of your curves like I've been dreaming about?"

Yeah, that was more like it. Except now she was having just

the teensiest moment of worrying the second he got her clothes off he would be disappointed.

She had great boobs, sure. That came with the territory and he'd already seen those. More than once, he'd mentioned her ass, and Gal's was a whole lot bigger than Kim Kardashian's. She was no swimsuit model. She had stretch marks and cellulite and -oh crap - had on granny panties instead of the pretty lingerie she'd wanted to wear the first time they got naked together.

Was she going to let a pair of ugly underpants ruin her sexy-times? Or spend the night alone because what those panties covered wasn't up to society's beauty standards? She might. If the man looking down at her was anyone else.

The way his eyes glowed with his hidden wolf inside, the way he licked his lip, and sucked it between his teeth while staring at her mouth, and especially the way he was patiently waiting for her to say yes, helped her get over her worries. "Talk dirty to me like that, my big bad wolf, and you can lick anything you want."

She pulled her hands out of his grasp and grabbed his shirt, yanking it over his head, wanting so much to feel his skin against hers. Gal pressed her fingers against the nearest muscle that clearly needed stroking. "You are incredibly hot, do you know that? What are you doing with a girl like me?"

Shit. Gal yanked her hand away and grimaced. She had not meant that last part to come out of her mouth. She absolutely did not want to screw this up by letting him see her insecurities. She was already fighting against the curse of the granny panties, she needed to at least pretend she was a confident sexy woman. That's what guys wanted, so said Cosmo. "Forget I said that."

"Nope. Not gonna let that slide. I'll tell you what I'm doing, not with a girl like you, but with you." He propped himself up on one arm and grabbed the hand she'd balled up into a fist. One by one, he slowly opened her fingers, and pressed a kiss to her palm. He put her hand back on his chest, where it had been before and covered it with his own. "What I'm doing is getting my mind completely fucking blown, by nothing more than a touch."

Max dragged her hand down his six-thousand pack abs, past the button of his jeans, twisting their hands so she was cupping the tree branch he must have hidden behind his zipper. No branch didn't do it justice. Log? Tree trunk? Sequoia? He sucked in a sharp breath and groaned.

"Feel how fucking hard I am for you? My cock has been aching to get out since before dinner. Because of you. You're still completely clothed and if I didn't have so much experience controlling my raging libido around you, I probably already would have come in my goddamned shorts just from finally having you in my bed."

The horrible mean girls in her head screamed it didn't matter who was in his bed, he'd be hot and horny because he knew he was getting laid. A smarter voice said that Max had trusted her with his deepest secret, had made himself vulnerable to her, and no one else. The smart girl said she and Max had something special and only a dummy would throw that away. Gal always was smart. The mean girls could fuck off.

She licked her lips and took a leap of smart faith. "What do you think would happen to you and your cock if we did take my clothes off?"

Max's eyes went incredibly dark and sparkly and his voice came out on a husky growl. "I think I wouldn't be able to resist burying myself in you, making you come over and over, so that your hot wet cunt squeezes and milks my cock of every last drop of cum I have until we're both so satisfied we can't remember why we didn't do this earlier."

The inner muscles of Gal's pussy squeezed getting all excited to do everything he'd said. "Then as soon as you grab a condom, we should probably take my clothes off and see if that's what happens. Because I bet you're right."

Gal gave his extra-large package a squeeze and moved to take off her shirt. Even if Max didn't have any protection, she knew better than to rely on anyone else and had a small discreet pack in her bag with three condoms in it. She hoped that would be enough. Although, she kind of hoped it wasn't near enough too.

Max didn't move. "I have condoms in my wallet, and I'll get them if you want me to. I thought you might. I'll wear a goddamned parka if it means I get to see you naked, I swear. But since you're already in on my true nature, you should know that wolves don't get diseases. Not like humans. So I can't give you any sexually transmitted diseases and you can't give me any either."

Gal sat up slightly and pushed herself up on her elbows. "Like, you don't get sick at all?"

He shook his head being completely serious. "Not even a cold."

"That's so not fair." She feigned pouting, but it was seriously pretty amazing. No wonder some wolves thought humans were so weak.

Max rubbed his scruffy chin against hers again. "The rules of fair play do not apply in love and war."

"Aww. You could definitely get in my pants with more accurately quoted sixteenth century poems."

"I'll remember that."

"I'll buy that you're clean and aren't going to give me some weird wolfy STD, but there's still that sticky business of babies. I'm not on any sort of hormonal birth control."

"Wolf-shifter pups can only be conceived under a full moon, and the cycle doesn't start for two more nights."

"You're making that up."

"Out of everything that you've seen tonight and has happened, that's what you think isn't real? I swear to you that it is. If we weren't on the verge of having hot and heavy sex, I'd say go ask my mom. But as I'm pretty sure I already have indents from the zipper of my jeans all up and down my cock from it trying to bust out, I ask that you believe me."

"I've never had sex without a condom before. Have you?"

"Do you really want me to answer that?"

"No. Maybe later. No. Pretend the last three seconds didn't happen and I said something sex-kitten like instead and you said something dirty and we decided the next best thing to do was rip off all of our clothes and get busy."

Max chuckled and kissed Gal, softly sliding his smiling lips across hers. "Then that's exactly what happened and we should commence with the clothes ripping."

He pushed the hem of her shirt up and over her head, where she had to help get it off her arms. When she had her head back out, the look on Max's face was so filled with lust her pussy clenched again. If her body was doing this with only his looks, she was probably going to die of pleasure when he actually touched her.

"Moon above, you're beautiful." Max bent his head and

pressed a soft kiss right over her heart. He nibbled his way back up her chest and to her collarbone. "I want you so badly, *kiska*."

"Then take me. You have me." She wrapped her hands into his hair and bared her neck to him, loving the way his teeth scraped across her skin. "That feels incredible. Do that some more."

Max jumped off the bed, breathing hard, and pulled at the button of his pants. He yanked them down his legs, taking his boxers with them.

She wasn't wrong when she'd said sequoia earlier. Holy cow, he was effing huge. Like how was that even going to fit, huge. Gulp.

Max reached for her jeans and she shoved his hands away. "It'll take longer if you do it. Let me."

She hadn't even taken her shoes off yet. She kicked them to the floor and wriggled around to get her jeans off, decided she looked and felt ridiculous and stood up, shucking them the same way he had. Expect she didn't take her granny panties with.

Oops. She had meant to. He didn't need to see the stripes and flowers in the briefs covering more skin than not. She reached for them and he was the one who stopped her this time. "Let me."

He ran his fingers along the elastic and dipped inside, cupping her ass. "I'm pretty sure I'm never going to be able to see any piece of clothing with tiny pink flowers on it ever again without getting hard as a fucking rock."

Gal closed her eyes half from embarrassment and half from the way he was running his fingers down along the seam of her rear end, creeping his way toward the danger zone.

"Can you please just take them off and hide them, never to be seen again?"

He snuck another hand inside the back of her panties. "Not a chance. I'm keeping these."

The fact that both his big hands fit inside of the fabric was the last straw. "I thought you were some kind of alpha male who could rip my undies off."

Rrrippp.

"Like that?" He threw the shreds over his shoulder.

"Ouch. Yes." That would teach her to challenge him. Teach her to do it all the damn time. Because while it kinda hurt to have one's panties ripped off, it was still pretty fricking hot that he'd done it.

"Here, let me kiss it and make it better." Max dropped to his knees, grabbed her inner thighs and buried his face in her thatch of curls. He spread open her pussy lips and licked right across her clit. "Mmm. You're fucking delicious, like sweet, ripe peaches. You're so wet and I'm going to lap up every drop."

Gal's hands pushed into his hair without her even telling them too. She wanted his mouth on her, but she wanted to get to taste him too. Oh boy, his tongue pressed against her clit in just the right way. She'd taste him in a minute. "Oh Max, yes."

Her legs wobbled a little as he pushed her higher and higher. Then they outright shook. Another minute of having him lick and suck and her knees were going to give out under her. They'd end up in a pile on the floor. She gripped his hair tight and tried to hang on. She might have too if he hadn't made that damn sexy low growling sound. Hearing him actually enjoy going down on her was more than she could handle.

Gal threw her head back and groaned through her orgasm, her legs gave out, and her body went into overload. Luckily, she didn't end up on the floor on top of Max squishing him to death as reward for his talented tongue. Max held her tight against the bed and continued to suck every last pulsating beat of her body's release from her.

Instead of ending up as a puddle on the floor, Max gave her the tiniest of shoves and she collapsed back on the bed, him still between her legs. He spread them even wider, gave one of her lower lips the softest of bites and worked his way up her body, kissing and nipping and caressing every inch of her along the way.

"I like seeing you this way, all relaxed and glowing. I'll have to make sure I give you lots of orgasms every night just so I can enjoy the sight of you all satisfied like this." He laid down next to her and ran his fingers in a soft caress up and down her neck and jaw.

She floated in that blissful afterglow for another minute before opening her eyes. "Is it a werewolf thing to be really good at doing that? Because I think you made me come in like twenty-seven seconds flat."

Max grinned down at her. "Maybe a bit longer than that. It's not a werewolf thing. It's a you and me thing."

"Hmm. We should test that theory out. Shall we see how long it takes me to get you off?" Gal licked her lips and Max sucked in a long breath.

"I want very little more than to see these pretty pink lips wrapped around my cock. I think if you even made kissy noises in the general vicinity of my lower half I'd probably explode. What I want even more is to be inside of you, fucking you so deep I don't know where I end and you begin.

I want to make you mine. My scent mingled with yours so that no other man or wolf has any question that we belong together."

Gal's heart skipped a beat. Did he really think they belonged together? Like forever? She was getting ahead of herself. She rolled to her side so she was facing him and wrapped one leg over his. "Yes, Max. Fuck me. Make me yours."

DIRTIER TALK

*W*anting Galyna was like wanting his next breath of air, a drink of water from a cool stream after a long hard hunt, like needing to raise his face to the sky and howl at the moon. Now that he had her under him, she consumed him completely. If he never touched another woman, hell even looked at another woman again, he would be happy.

If he believed that wolves had fated mates, there was no doubt in his mind, his body, his soul, that she was his. He didn't need any ceremony under the full moon to know they belonged together. He sure as hell hoped she felt the same because after tonight, he was never letting her go.

His pack was going to have to deal with that. Something he would worry about later. Now the only thing he needed to concern himself with was how many times he could get her to come screaming his name. She'd lit up with desire at the way he talked to her with the frank words about what he wanted to do with her.

"You want me to fuck you, do you?" He kissed her neck, nipping at the spot that his wolf begged to bite.

"Fast and hard," he scraped his teeth across her skin, and gave her tiny bites across the soft flesh of her breasts. "...or slow and gentle?"

He sucked one of her small taut nipples into his mouth and swirled his tongue around it the same way he'd teased her clit. The other one needed the same attention. He wouldn't want it to feel left out. Gal arched her back, pushing into him and moaning. Just the way he wanted her, wet and wanting. "Either way, you're coming at least ten more times tonight."

Her eyes went doe-eyed wide. Her voice came out as a squeak. "Ten?"

She cleared her throat and narrowed her eyes. "I mean, ten? You think so, huh?"

So fucking adorable. She was trying so hard to give him this confident sexy side, but he was loving the shy, surprised girl under the facade. He didn't even know how much experience she had. He didn't really want to either. She wasn't a virgin, his senses told him that much. He almost felt like he should treat her as such though. If he had his way, they'd have plenty of time to get really dirty. Tonight should be something special.

"Hmm. I know so." He licked each of her nipples again and then blew cool air on them. They went from plump to pebbled and hard in an instant. "Why don't we make it an even dozen."

She cleared her throat. "How many of those are yours?"

God, she made him laugh. He'd never been inches from putting his dick in any other woman and laughed as much as he did with her. Sex was about, well, sex. Fucking, making sure his partner came, making sure he did. It had never been the fun and games he was playing with Gal. This was a hell of a lot hotter and twice as fun. "Are you questioning my virility, kiska? I'll have you know wolves have plenty of stamina."

"So..., what?" She raised an eyebrows and got a naughty little grin, finally relaxing. "Like two?"

He'd banter with her half the night if that's what made her comfortable. They'd get to the sex. It was the getting there that was half the fun. "You want to share your orgasms with me? I'll take, hmm, let's start small, and you can give me four."

"We're going to need snacks." Such a minx. Her eyes twinkled so perfectly. He could almost see the sparking of the moon in them.

"I think I'll be plenty satisfied snacking on you." He gently pushed her head aside and he meant to kiss his way to her ear and tease her. Instead he lingered over the pulse point in her throat. His wolf's fangs wanted to descend, to mark her skin, claiming her as his mate. He had to push that urge back down. She'd only found out about his true nature today. She wasn't ready for a wolf mating.

He pulled in a shuddered breath and licked the spot he wanted to sink his teeth into. Soon, he promised the wolf. It might be a lie to placate them both. It might be the only way he made it through the night without claiming her. Max blinked a few times before lifting his head again. Gal had gone quiet, but not still. Her chest still rose and fell faster than normal as she breathed hard with arousal, and his own heart beat as fast as hers.

"How about we each start with one, together." Gal reached up and stroked his face.

Yeah. There was his sweet, sexy girl. Her touch was the

signal he'd been waiting for to show that she was relaxed and ready. She'd never decided on how she wanted him, so he picked for them. He'd thought their first time together would be hot and heavy, but no. Taking his time, giving all of himself to her, that's what his soul needed. To be one with her.

Max moved over her, caging her under him, and putting his hard muscles in line with her lush curvy body. With one knee he opened her thighs and reached between them. Max stroked the inside of her thigh, and caressed his way up to her pussy. She was wet enough that her juices already coated her skin, her body more than ready for his.

She closed her eyes and pushed her head back into the soft blanket, welcoming his touch. "Yes, Max. You know how to touch me."

He pushed his fingers into her wet warmth and she clenched around him, her body begging him for more. Her body flushed with each slide of his fingers in and out of her, looking for exactly the right spot to drive her crazy. When she gripped the sheets in her fists, he knew he'd found it.

"Oh, yes. Right there. Please, more Max."

Her wish was his command. He swirled his thumb around her clit and crooked his fingers to caress her g-spot. She was coming apart for him, and only him. He could still smell her arousal, but in this new more intimate moment, it changed from the ripe fruit that drove him crazy to something even more intoxicating.

He couldn't put a name to the scent of her emotions. Something in between peaches and licorice, sunshine and rain, the muskiness of a humid night in the forest and a lazy Sunday morning. She was perfectly intoxicating and all he'd ever wanted.

Love. She smelled of love.

The little hairs all along his arms stood up, doing the wave. He'd fucking fallen in love with her.

He didn't know when or how. He definitely knew he shouldn't have. There was no going back now. His heart would forever be hers. The words were on the tip of his tongue to say, but he didn't say them. Tonight he would show her how he felt. Tomorrow, or the next day, when there weren't so many new revelations about who and what he was, then he'd tell her.

"Max, I need you," she whispered in a soft, husky voice. "Please."

"I need you too." He had to swallow down the knot of emotions welling up in his throat. He wasn't even inside of her yet, and this was already the most passionate meaningful sexual experience of his life.

He leaned in and took her mouth in a slow, deep kiss, putting all the words and emotions into the message from his body to hers. She wrapped her arms around his neck and moaned into his mouth.

His cock was already notched at her entrance and he wanted to come so badly, he had to concentrate like an untried kid not to embarrass himself. He would not come before she did. He would not. Gal would always, always come first. In bed and in his life.

He slowly pushed into her and his head nearly exploded from the pleasure. No sex had ever been this good. Not with anyone else, ever. This wasn't sex, this was a fucking epiphany.

"Oh Max, holy... Max, you feel... I can't...don't stop." Gal wrapped her legs around the back of his and tugged him closer. "I don't know what kind of move you're doing, but do. not. stop."

"I won't, baby." If she thought this was a move, he'd better get his real moves going. He wanted to blow her mind as much as she was his. "We're just getting started."

He pistoned his hips so he filled her and she groaned. That was the sound he wanted to hear. It was practically killing him to go this slow but he would keep up exactly this pace if it meant he could continue to see her like this. He withdrew from her feeling every centimeter of her body sliding against his.

"Please, Max, more." She dug her nails into his shoulders, gripping him hard. "You're killing me. Faster, harder, take me."

Thank God. Max thrust into her and set up a rhythm that had them both panting. He wasn't going to last long like this. But Gal was on fire too. He simply needed to find just the right way to push her over the edge. Their bodies were doing what they both needed, but his dick and her pussy weren't the only erogenous zones on their bodies.

In fact, he knew the best one, and the best way. Words were this sexy librarian's jam. She'd already shown him how much she was turned on when he talked dirty to her. And he was one dirty fucker.

She was about to find out exactly how dirty he was.

"Galyna, *kriska*, you're hot little cunt has my cock so hard. I can't fucking wait to come inside of you, pushing my seed deep into you." Dirty, yes, Also completely true. He almost wished it was the full moon and he could put a baby into her belly right now. She would be even more beautiful, plump and round with his child.

Now was not a good time to bring a new child into the pack. By god. He was going to mate and marry this woman. Together they would have an amazing family. Later.

"Max, I love how dirty you are. More." Gal's nails strafed down his arms as he pushed into her again and again.

"You're a greedy girl and I love it. You're going to come for me, aren't you?"

"Yes, mmm, yes."

"Because this pussy is mine, you're mine." Max grabbed her arms and pushed them over her head again. That thrust her breasts up at him and his mouth watered to taste her again. "Say you're mine, Galyna."

"I want to be yours." A thin bead of sweat trickled down from her hair and dropped from her ear to her shoulder. "Only yours."

That small droplet was too tempting and he had to bend his head and lick it up. "Good girl. This cunt is mine now."

The saltiness exploded on his tongue like pop rocks. He needed so much more. Max sucked on her earlobe and licked that sensitive spot behind her ear. That still wasn't enough.

The fangs of his wolf elongated and there was no stopping them this time. With every thrust into Gal's tight cunt his wolf took more control. This was a claiming by his beast. She was his mate and the whole pack would know. "Your body is mine. I'm going to take you in every way I can. I'll fuck your pussy, your tits, your mouth, your ass. Because they are all mine now."

"Yes. Yours. Max. Max. I'm so close. Please, I need you, I need to come."

His mouth watered with the need to bite her neck, mark

her with the imprint of his teeth so no other man or wolf would ever even think about touching what belonged to him. His wolf pushed him to do it. There was no resisting. Max let the wolf rise up. His eyes shifted, letting him see every little detail of her hair and skin. His hearing amplified and he reveled in the sound of their bodies slapping together and her whimpers of pleasure. He kept his claws reigned in so as not to scratch her, but he was on the edge of his control and that was the best he could do.

The wolf took control. It understood that this woman was human and needed a human mating, but it would push the edge, melding human and wolf. It pushed her head aside making her neck open and vulnerable to him. He snarled dark and menacingly, challenging her, testing her submission to him. "Mine."

"Yes, yes. Yours." Her cunt squeezed him and her orgasm fluttered right on the edge.

Her body begged him to take her into the climax. Max and his wolf, one, together took her body and sank his teeth into the soft flesh of her neck. She bucked beneath him and screamed out his name, not in pain, but total nirvana. Her pussy clenched and spasmed, her muscles contracting and milking his cock, pulling him toward the climax with her.

He slammed into her body, no longer able to control his thrusts. His teeth sank in harder and his cock pulsed, growing even bigger until the wolf's knot at the base was bulging and ready to lock him inside of her. He thrust forward one last time, pushing deeper than before, notching his cock inside of her. They were locked together. The wolf growled around the flesh of her in his mouth claiming Gal as his own.

The muscles of his stomach bunched and Max's orgasm

started deep inside. His balls drew up and the pleasure of coming into her willing pussy completely overwhelmed him. They were intertwined, her arms and legs thrown around him to hold him to her. His mouth keeping her in place and his cock snugly fit as if their bodies were made for each other. He finally was able to release her from his bite and roared out her name, repeating it over and over, intermingled with the wolf's claim of mine.

His body strained to drain every last drop of semen from him and he collapsed, rolling onto his side with Gal still tightly gripped in his hold so he wouldn't crush her beneath him. They floated together in the hot afterglow of their love-making, their bodies still secured together.

She laid her head on his chest, breathing hard and holding him tight. Tiny aftershocks of her climax shook her, squeezing him, drawing both of their orgasms out. Slowly their bodies gave in and the grip they had on each other loosened. His wolf slowly receded, satisfied it had made its claim and marked its mate.

His cock wasn't quite ready to let go yet. Max stroked one hand up and down her back, soothing her and whispered softly into her ear. "That was amazing, love. You were amazing."

She didn't move except for another soft clench of her inner muscles around his dick. "Mmmrrrmmmrr."

"God, you still feel so good. I never want to leave the heat of your pussy." He couldn't yet even if he wanted to. The wolf's knot at the base of his cock hadn't yet gone down and their bodies were forced together until it did. He didn't mind even a little.

Her face was smashed against his chest, but she waved her hand at him in a go away- not now motion. "Nrrph nrr."

Max wrapped a few strands of her hair around his hand and gave her a very gentle tug. "*Kiska*, are you all right?"

"Ooph." She lifted her face from his chest. "Mmm-hmm. I think all those orgasms turned my brain to mush because you made me forget how to talk for a minute there. Am I speaking English now? Can you understand me?"

He understood exactly how she felt. Max loved this silly, relaxed side of her that had shown up. He would happily play along. "*Nyet. Ya ne znayu.*"

She sighed and laid her head back down. "It's official. My brain is mush, which means I died. You killed me. With your dick. And now I'm dead which is why I can't speak correctly and you can't understand me and I can't understand you, and I would not have wanted to go any other way."

"Being inside of you is definitely heaven." Her needless insecurities from before were gone and good riddance to them. She had no idea how sexy she was and he was going to keep her all to himself.

Fuck yeah he was, his wolf agreed. The moment he'd called her his replayed in his head. Mine. Mine. Mine.

Gal drew lazy circles on his chest and arms, following the lines of his tattoos. "I guess you died too. The afterlife must have a universal translator."

He took a peek at her neck and couldn't wait to see what became of the mark he'd made there. Now it was still swollen and red. The circular bite of his wolf would heal quick enough and turn into a unique mark representing him. Seeing the bite appeased his wolf and the knot locking their bodies together eased allowing him to pull out if he wanted to.

He didn't. Max kissed her neck gently. When they were both recovered he would show it to her. She would either love it, or hate it. Love him or leave him. Shit, he hoped his wolf was right.

She felt right in his arms, in his bed, in his head. "Your mind is a wondrous thing. I'm the one barely breathing and forming coherent words."

She popped back up and grinned at him. "Really?"

"Do you think I would still be buried deep inside of you, my dick hard as a fucking diamond, if that wasn't the best sex ever?" He moved his hips precisely to demonstrate that fact. She still felt so fucking tight if he did much more of this, he'd be fucking her again in no time.

She bit her lip and made a sound that was somewhere between a squeal and a moan. Then Gal gave as good as she got, pushing forward to meet his. "Ever?"

Max was the one moaning this time. "Ever."

He grabbed her hips and moved so she straddled him, sitting right on his cock. A light breeze blew the curtains and beams of moonlight streamed into the room. His Galyna was so beautiful, she practically glowed in the light. Just like that he needed her again. "I want to see you come on my dick. I want to watch you play with your tits while I thumb your clit. Let me see you come apart for me."

Gal licked her lips and tentatively rocked her hips.

"Fuck. Do that again, baby. You're the one who is going to turn my brain to mush." He wrapped his hands under her ass and helped her move up and down on his cock.

It only took her a few glides to get her own rhythm and she closed her eyes and brought her hands up to her breasts, playing and tugging at her nipples. Oh, yeah. As promised, he reached between her thighs and found that sensitive button, stroking it. "Ride me, Galyna. Ride me hard, all night."

And she did.

*W*ow. Just... wow.

If that was what sex was, whatever she'd been doing under the covers, in the dark, with boys before had been, like, she didn't know. Teeter-totter or something. But not sex.

She'd felt things with Max she'd never even fathomed before. And she didn't mean the orgasms. Although, those were unbelievable. The magazines talked about full body orgasms, but they didn't even have a fricking clue. It was like her mind and body had become the very goddess of sex and pleasure herself. Everything she'd given to Max, she'd received back tenfold.

Then they'd done it all again. And again.

Both of them should be completely exhausted, but Gal was exhilarated. Every cell and molecule of her body tingled with delight and energy. She could run a marathon. Or have marathon sex.

She could also lay here in Max's arms and talk with him for hours more. They'd talked half the night. The half that they weren't boinking like bunnies. Now the early morning light filtered in the window. It had to end sometime. She hated the night to be over. But, also, she had to pee and she was going to eat an entire hippopotamus for breakfast.

Max's stomach rumbled before hers did and that made her laugh. "I told you we should have had snacks."

"Next time I'll be sure to stock up. Giving you ten orgasms is quite the workout." He patted his stomach.

Like he even needed to work out. He already had more than six-pack abs. He thought he was hot shit, he didn't need his ego inflated at all. "It wasn't ten."

Max raised an eyebrow challenging her statement silently. Man it was fun to flirt with him like this. Naked.

She'd never been that comfortable without her clothes on before, during, or after sex with any other guy she'd been with. Being with Max though, she didn't mind sharing her vulnerabilities with him.

Gal stuck out her tongue at him. "It was eleven. So there."

"Bring that tongue over here. I can think of a lot more things for you to do with it than that." He grabbed for her and she squealed dodging him. She had no doubt he and his wolfy reflexes could catch her if he wanted to. His heart-melting smile showed he was having as much fun playing this game with her as she was with him.

She'd definitely be doing lots more things with her tongue. But later. She really did have to pee. Gal scooted off the end of the bed before he could grab her. "Yes, and we can do all of them after I get to go to the little girls room and you feed me."

He fake rolled his eyes. "You're so demanding. Which is really fucking hot, by the way."

"Sweet talker." Gal grabbed the blanket and wrapped it

around herself exactly like the way she'd seen women do it in the movies. Her reality was rapidly becoming way cooler than any made up story. She crossed toward the bedroom's en suite bathroom, but paused two steps past a picture on the wall in a frame with glass.

Something strange had been reflected there. Gal backed up and moved her head to the left and her shoulder closer to the reflection. "Holy mother, what is that?"

This was no mere hickey. She reached up and gently touched the red circle of skin. Pleasurable tingles, not pain, sparkled through the wound when she ran her fingers over it. Before she could even blink, Max was behind her, watching her warily.

"Did this happen when we were," she waved at the bed. "I remember you biting me, but I thought you were just giving me a hickey. This is..."

"It will heal, quickly. It won't look like that for more than a few more hours. I'm not sure how long though because I've only ever seen them on a wolftress. Your human ability to heal is different from ours otherwise it would have already transformed." Max's words were hurried, anxious, and filled with concern. He skimmed his fingers over hers, not quite touching the mark, only her.

"Babe," she put as much awe and excitement into her question as she could mostly to soothe his nerves. She turned her hand and grasped his. "Am I going to turn into a werewolf?"

His body language relaxed instantly. "No. Well. I don't know exactly what's going to happen. It's forbidden for wolves to bite humans. It's our greatest taboo."

"You guys have a lot of rules that we're breaking." The

consequences would come, but she refused to worry about them now. She would live in this moment.

He nodded. "Yes. Because this is more than a bite." Max swallowed and pressed a kiss to the circle of faded teeth marks. "This is a mate's bite. A mark that shows that you are mine."

His.

They had said the words in the heat of the moment. She hadn't wanted it to be just another form of dirty talk. She'd meant it when he asked her to declare that she was his. No way did she think he meant it beyond the bed. That was a silly fantasy.

Except it wasn't.

Say you're mine, Galyna.

The tingles she'd felt around the bite mark spread, rushing over her skin and raising little goosebumps everywhere. She was his and he was hers.

Gal spun on her heels, grabbed Max around the neck, completely dropping the blanket, and pulled him down for a soul-deep kiss. He must have been surprised by her reaction because at first his lips were frozen and she had to coax him into letting her tongue in. It only took him a second to click on and he wrapped his arms around her back and kissed her back with as much fervor.

Between mashing their faces together, Max whispered against her lips, "You aren't mad?"

She smiled against his mouth and nipped at his lower lip. "Nope."

Max swept her off her feet and back to the bed. "Not freaking out?"

He was crazy if he thought she was going to be upset.

She'd won the freaking hot guy who loves me jackpot. Who cared whether he was a wolf or a donkey or a saber-toothed bunny rabbit, as long as he loved her and she loved him. "Not even a little."

"God, you're amazing." He crawled over her like he had last night, caging her in between his arms and his body again.

She didn't want to be anywhere else.

"Amazing in bed." She crooked a finger at him.

Max spread her legs open with his knees and reached between them, finding her clit like the master of her body. "Yes, you are."

Before they could get going a knock sounded on the door. Max growled and glared at the offending sound. "Go away. We're busy."

"I'm sure you are, dear. But I need the two of you to get dressed and come out here. Now." Selena's voice did not have that same calm it had last night.

Gal stifled a giggle. "I think we're in trouble."

Max frowned and his eyes flitted back and forth for a moment before he looked back down at her. "I don't think that's it. My mother knew exactly what she was doing, throwing us together. She practically told me to fuck you. Who do you think lit all those candles? No. This is something else."

Okay. That must be a wolf-shifter thing. No way her own parents even wanted to know she'd ever kissed a boy much less encouraged her to have sex. They wanted her to get married and have kids, sure, but they'd prefer if she never saw a man's penis if she could help it.

"Sorry to cut this short, kiska. We'd better go see what's going on. With my father away, I need to make sure the pack is protected and safe." He rolled off the bed and gathered their clothes off the floor. He handed her everything except for the shredded pair of underpants that were suspiciously missing.

Maybe later she could get another pack of clothing from Selena with new undergarments. That whole having clothes ready in case of emergency shifting was a smart idea and she'd be making up some packs of her own. Which would also be good in case of emergency sexy times. Of which she hoped to have many. "It's okay. We have lots more nights ahead of us."

"I hope we do, love. I hope we do." Max gave her a quick kiss and yanked on his jeans and t-shirt while she ran to the bathroom to finally pee. When she was fully clothed, if going commando and free-boobing it counted, he led her back down the hall to the main part of the house.

They found Selena, Kosta, and a huge guy she sort of recognized from town sitting around the kitchen table. The man was breathing hard as if he'd run a marathon and he was pale as death. His clothes were torn with what looked like claw marks. Through one of the larger tears in his shirt, Gal saw angry-looking wounds.

A lump formed in her chest and she quietly bit her finger to stave off a gasp. Max squeezed her hand quickly but then released her and clapped the man on the shoulder. "Aleksei, what's happened?"

Doc, the local vet walked in from the kitchen with a mug of something and handed it to the guy. "Give him a second. He needs to drink the theriac before he does anything else."

Aleksei took the mug and tipped it back gulping the drink down so fast dribbles of yellowish thick liquid dripped down his face and beard. Whatever was in that gooey concoction had at least the effect of letting Aleksei catch his breath.

"Theriac? What the hell is going on here?" Max glanced between his mother and Doc.

Selena answered first. "Wolfsbane. The bastards."

"Who?" Max growled.

Gal jumped when Aleksei slammed the mug down on the table. He wiped his mouth and face with the back of his hand. He took a slow breath and answered. "The Grimms intercepted us before we even got outside of Bay County. They've already got the next three closest packs on their side. They are amassing an army to move against us and anyone who allies under the Troika banner."

"Shit. I didn't think Crescent pack would turn against us too." Kosta got up and paced back and forth. "Fucking Niko."

Gal didn't understand what their eldest brother had to do with this. She did think he should be here to help his family with this nightmare. Not to mention whatever was going on with Zara. She was going to read that boy the riot act when he got back from wherever the hell he was.

Aleksei shook his head and took several more labored breaths. "There's some crazy-ass shit going down, Maxsim. They've got these three women with creepy dead eyes who made us want to drink their poison. I've never seen anything like it."

Max glanced over at his brother and then his mom. "Like Key. They may also have been forced into mated submission. We need to find out more about the women they are choosing. If they have inherent powers we need to find out who they might target in Rogue."

Max flicked his eyes to Gal. She figured they were both wondering if this had anything to do with Zara's disappearance.

"Aleksei. Where's my father?"

This injured man, who'd fought for his life looked as though Max's simple question had struck him like a death blow to the heart.

"They sent me back to give you a warning." Aleksei took a faltering breath. "The Crescent Alpha is claiming our territory and pack because of his defeat of your father. Which is bullshit. They took his life without honor."

Selena grabbed her throat. "Piotr is dead?"

"If they hadn't drugged me with the wolfsbane and their witchy women hadn't messed with my mind. They wouldn't have been able to make me run from them. I swear I tried to stay and fight." The big tough guy's voice wavered and he went down on one knee before Max. "They chased me through three states before I figured out how to make my way back here. I would have fought them if I could, Alpha. I have failed the Troikas and I only hope you will allow me to say goodbye to my beloved before you kill me."

Alpha? Gal was under the impression that Max's older brother would become the alpha. That lump in her stomach suddenly grew a good three times in size.

Max stumbled back and she caught his hand. She gave it a squeeze just like he'd done for her a moment ago, letting him know she was there for him. He glanced down at her, the wolf already glowing in his eyes.

He shook his head, shock straining his face, confirming her own fear. Kosta also had that look of shock and awe, and when Gal glanced over at Selena she had a tired, sad resignation to her face. Max closed his eyes and clenched his jaw, the muscles there pulsing. "You won't be killed, Aleksei. Not by my hand, nor my order. You have served us as well as you could. I will not take you away from your loved ones. We're going to need all the wolf power we can muster in the upcoming days, I fear."

Aleksei bowed his head. "Thank you, Alpha."

"If Doc clears you, go to your family now. Spend as much time with them as you can today. I'll call on you soon to get more information about Crescent turning on us. Anything you can remember might help."

Aleksei rose and Doc gave him a once over. "You're recovering fine, but I think you could use another dose of my theriac. I'd like to see your wolf heal those wounds on your back."

"I'll help you mix it up then, shall I?" Selena stood and waved the two men toward the kitchen. She gave long meaningful looks to both Max and Kosta that Gal guessed meant they would do their grieving in private later.

She would stay for Max if they'd allow that, do anything that needed to be done. For this one horrible moment, she simply held his hand tight so that he would know she was here.

As soon as the three people were out of the room, Kosta stood and paced in front Max. "This has to end, brother. We can't allow those one-blood Grimm bastards to out us to the whole fucking world. That's their plan, you know? They're fucking glad Niko offed the Tzar. It was the excuse they needed to break every goddamned law we have. While you were off fucking around, I actually did my duty to the pack and gathered some intel."

In a blink Max left Gal's side and had Kosta up against the wall, his hand wrapped around his younger brother's throat. "Be careful how you talk about my mate, Konstantin."

Kosta thrashed, but couldn't budge from Max's grip. Gal's heart rate skyrocketed and an uncomfortable surge of adrenaline washed over her. Here came those consequences.

"Your mate? You can't fucking be serious. She's a human."

Oh, okay. Gal saw how it was now. Kosta was the one fucking around. Heli might say it was nothing more than a fling, but she was going to be devastated. His reaction also meant she and Max's lives were about to get a lot stickier too. She didn't a hundred percent understand what being his mate meant or the new alpha would be. But if most wolf-shifters felt the way Kosta did, her relationship with Max was going to be a roadblock for them all.

She should give him up. Make a promise to forget about them, their kind, and walk away. She should let Max do whatever his new duties were without her being a chain around his shoulders, weighing him down. She should. But she didn't know if she could.

"Yes. My mate. And in a few days, under the full moon, she will become the pack matriarch. So I suggest you learn how to show some respect."

Unless she wasn't around in a few days.

Kosta finally jerked out of Max's grip and snarled. His eyes were glowing, not that same blue that Max had, but with a darker almost purple light. "It's a good thing dad and Niko are dead. Because it would kill them to see you destroy this pack."

Zara was going to be shattered.

"Niko would understand." Max said so quietly, it was almost a whisper except for the growl beneath it.

"Niko left her, Max. He went to serve the Tzar as penance for wanting her in the first place. That's what got him killed. You know, I know it, and pretty damn soon, the whole of

Wolfkind is going to find out we're not a powerful wolf pack. We're a joke."

Two pillows flew past Gal's face and right into the faces of Max and Kosta.

"No, *malysh*." Selena stood next to a couch with three other matching pillows. "We are the change the wolf-shifter world needs."

SACRIFICES

*F*uck.

If there was anyone Max needed on his side, who expected to understand, it was Kosta. He wasn't sure who else would support his relationship with Gal besides his mother. It would have been nice to have the best of the Enforcers on his side too. But his little fit and storming out when Selena had intervened was an eye-opener to Max.

Thank the moon and stars he had already marked and claimed Galyna. He had a feeling he was going to need her to be his rock.

"Give him some time to cool off. He and your father didn't always have the best relationship. This is going to be hardest on him." His mother crossed an arm, folding in on herself.

He was such a dumbass. Her mate had just been killed, her world even more upended than his own. "I'm sorry, mother. I shouldn't have reacted to him and started a fight. The two of us should be the ones there for you right now, not the other way around."

"We all need to pull together. This pack had taken blow after blow in the past few months and everything else, family squabbles and grieving all will have to be put aside. You're the one who has to lead these wolves now, Maxsim. No one else. You are the alpha."

"What if I'm not ready, mom?" Alphas weren't supposed to question themselves. They were strong, they were leaders, their word and will were law.

"You are, *malysh*. I wasn't kidding when I said we were going to be the change. Your father and I have known it since the three of you were born. He tried his best to ignore it and pretend everything was the status quo, but it never was and never would be. Niko set this shift in motion, you have to take the next turn."

Gal came to stand beside him and slipped her hand into his. Her simple gesture already soothed his beast that was itching to get out. "Does what your saying have anything to do with this?"

She pulled her collar aside and showed Selena her mark. Except it sure as hell wasn't the simple red bite mark he'd worried over an hour ago. His teeth marks were still visible, but only as they were incorporated into the blue glowing design of a full moon on her skin.

Selena stared at the mark, flicked her eyes to Max, and then wrapped Galyna into a giant hug. "Yes, it has everything to do with the fact that you two are fated mates."

When Selena released Gal, she grabbed Max by the cheeks and squeezed them as if he was a three-year-old pup. "I knew you would claim her. You just needed a little nudge."

"Mother." Max rolled his eyes, but smiled too. He didn't

understand how his mother knew Galyna was his fated mate or why she was good with him mating a human, but he appreciated that she was.

"Now, let's get to work. You need to call the pack in to announce your ascension to alpha, and declare your claim on Galyna. We were already preparing for the mating ceremony in a few nights, so that is in motion. You have explained what will happen at the ritual to her, didn't you, Max?"

Oh fuck. "You really think it's wise to go forward with the ceremony?"

"What's going to happen at the ritual? Ew, is it blood? Is there a sacrifice. I'm not ripping the head off a chicken, Max."

Selena patted Gal on the arm. "No blood. Unless you're a virgin, and after the ruckus you two made last night, we all know you're not."

"Mother." This was not how he wanted this conversation to go.

Gal turned about fifty shades of pink, which was both adorable and disconcerting. She was probably going to kick his ass later. "Oh man. You could hear us? Wait a second. What do you mean? Do you sacrifice virgins?"

The look of utter grotesque shock on Gal's face and her questions had Max scrambling. "No, love. The mating ceremony is about claiming for all to see. I'll bite you again, where you're marked, and... claim you."

Her eyes went wide and then narrowed at him. "Why do I have the feeling that claiming me doesn't involve a speech or a simple declaration like 'I do'?"

"What Max is trying to say is that you have to have sex." How the hell his mother said that so nonchalantly, he'd never know.

Gal waved toward the bedrooms. "We already have."

There was no way around this. He'd just have to tell her quick. Like shifting. A short, fast hit of pain and it would be over. "In front of the pack."

Her jaw dropped open and slowly her lips formed a sweet little 'oh.' The pink in her cheeks and on her chest went bright red. Max would be worried, except for the flicker of lust in her eyes as her pupils dilated. The ripe fruit scent of her arousal swirled between them. Christ. She was turned on by the idea. Maybe his sweet girl was dirtier than he thought.

They never did have that discussion about past lovers. Suddenly he found himself feeling pretty damn jealous. His wolf was panting for her and wanted to re-stake its claim on her, ensure no other man could hold any part of her mind or body. Max grabbed Gal around the waist and pulled her into his arms. He tipped her chin up and stared into her dark, sparkling eyes. "I will have the pack, the world, everyone, dammit, know you are mine, Galyna. But in the moment it will be only you and me, our bodies joined as one. It will be my hands, my mouth, my cock giving you pleasure. You will come for me and only me, and I for you."

She licked her lips and he felt her heart beating rapidly, her chest against his. She inhaled ragged breaths and nodded, the tiniest bobs of her head. "Okay."

Max kissed his mate long and hard, sweeping his tongue into her mouth. She groaned and wrapped her foot around the back of his leg. If their world wasn't on the verge of collapsing he'd take her back to bed right now. As it was he was already acutely aware of his mother patiently waiting for him to get his head out of his pants. Or rather out of Gal's pants as it were. He nipped at her lip and gave it a soft lick and then sadly, pulled away.

She rubbed a hand along his jaw. "You should know when this is over, you're buying me the biggest honking diamond ring."

He would buy her diamonds and pearls and anything else she wanted. He was totally gonna put a ring on it. "When this is over, you can have anything you want, my love."

Her smile lit up her whole face and his whole life. "I just want you, Max Troika."

"Aww," His mother cooed. "You two are almost sickly sweet. Wrap that feeling up in your mind because you're going to need it. What lies ahead is going to be a bitch and a half. I promise."

Leave it to his mother to bring them back to the reality of the situation. She was right, of course. That's what years of being the pack's matriarch had done. Made her the wisest women he knew.

That would be Gal someday too if they could make it through the next few battles. He could hardly wait to see her with their own children. Not that it was a good time to bring pups into the world. But someday they would. "I'm going to need you by my side for the next few days. If we're going to get the pack to accept you as the new matriarch we have to present a united front. Can you call in to work?"

If Max had his own way, he'd have her quit her job all together. He could take care of her financially. But he wasn't stupid. She'd worked hard for her education and was not the kind to want to be a kept woman. As long as he could protect her, he'd be satisfied. For now.

Gal made a cute thinking face, scrunching up her nose and pushing out her lips. "Umm. Let me see what I can do. I'm supposed to do story time this afternoon and close again this evening."

It took everything in him not to blurt out that he couldn't let her do that. "I can send a couple of enforcers with you for the afternoon, but I don't want you out after dark. If the Grimms and Crescents are going to attack, that's when they'll strike."

She tipped her head to the side and her eyes joined the array of features displaying her brain at work. "What if we let them?"

"Not a chance." He couldn't control it that time. He was not taking that kind of risk with her life. The second a wolf from any other pack got a whiff of her, they'd know she was with him.

"Now, hear me out. Selena said you need to call the pack in to tell them you're the alpha now. Wouldn't it be all intimidating and stuff if you did it right in front of them. Show them you aren't scared and that their harassment of the Troikas won't be tolerated."

Shit. It was a good plan. "You didn't happen to study military strategy along with your librarian degree, did you?"

"No. But I have read a lot of books. Including The Art of War. I have a few favorite quotes from Sun Tzu that I certainly never thought I'd apply to anything but learning how to get along with my dad. Definitely not for an actual war. But if the book fits, wear it."

His mother nodded with an eye trained on Max's very smart mate. "I like it. Let them follow Gal from the library to

Sleepy Folk. They won't suspect you even know about your father yet if we keep to our regular routines and hide Aleksei. I'll call Doc and your brother. Kosta could use a task to keep him occupied."

Max wondered if his father had gotten run over by the women in his life like he'd just been. Maybe that's what being an alpha was like. Listening to the good ideas of the people he trusted and letting them do what they do best. He had no doubt that with very little intervention from him, every wolf in Rogue would be at Sleepy Folk tonight already in on the plan.

"I have one other suggestion." Gal raised her hand like a kid in class who wasn't sure they had the right answer.

"You're on a roll. Lay it on me." She might not be confident in her idea, but Max already was. He already understood why having a strong matriarch for a pack was so vital.

Gal glanced over at his mother who gave her the go ahead nod. "I think you should let the other wolves who are in love with human women or men bring them tonight too."

Selena stopped in her tracks, but didn't say anything. She waited silently, telling him without words it was his call. He rubbed his jaw, stalling. Gal wasn't simply asking him to allow the wolves he already knew were seeing humans the same freedom he'd taken with her. She wanted him to take the next step.

They weren't ready. Kosta was proof of that. But if he brought Gal and presented her as his mate he would already be crossing the line into outlaw territory. He'd broken every law, rule, and taboo with her. When his mother had spoken of their world changing, Gal was the catalyst.

The plan was to present a strong united front. If he and Gal showed up together, with her marked and claimed to the new pack alpha, there was going to be dissent. More than that. Wolves weren't exactly known for polite disagreements. By a quick calculation in his head, he could lose a good half of the pack over this.

Instead of presenting an unassailable front to the other packs, he could be gifting them with a truckload of new members. That would put the pack in volatile jeopardy.

The wolf's intuition was much stronger than Max's alone. It knew what it had to do, Max simply had to let it. His gut told him that allowing his wolves to be the first to be able to claim their true mates, he would make the pack stronger. Wolves across the world who had been denied the same would come to be Troikas.

But the ones opposed, like the one-bloods, would declare all out war.

An alpha always did what was best for the pack, even if it wasn't what he wanted. "I don't think we're ready to let the entire town in on our secret."

"But--" Gal's face fell and she took a step away from him.

She had to understand the consequences of being a part of the pack. "Gal, I never had that same confidence that Niko did to outright defy my parents. I had my own rebellious streak, but it was tame human stuff. Until you. You bring out the best in me and that's fucking scary. I need you on my side if any of this is going to work."

She nodded, but he could see she was still upset.

"The world isn't ready to know that werewolves exist side by side with them. But I'm betting there are more humans in

Rogue that have already been entrusted with that secret and have proven themselves worthy. We're going to need them to stand as evidence that this shift in our culture isn't a mistake. We need you to be the first among them to step forward and give your fealty to the pack."

"You know that I will."

He never thought otherwise. His wolf had always known she was right for him, and the pack. "I do. I'm counting on that it will be enough to show those that will doubt us that love isn't our enemy. Let's make the calls and find out who has human mates."

Gal's face lit up. "I know who to call."

Max wasn't aware she knew any other men or women in his pack. Which meant she must know some other women who were seeing wolves. Some heads were going to get busted if his wolves hadn't impressed upon their partners the importance of secrecy. Maybe this wasn't a good idea.

"Your bartender, Harley." She pulled out her phone and flipped through her contacts.

Max knew he was being a hypocrite for thinking ill of his pack mate. He'd told Gal his secret after only a few days. Harley did have a girlfriend he'd been with a while. They even lived together. "You know his girlfriend? Does she know about us?"

"Don't get all growly with me. I don't know her at all." She put her hands on her hips Wonder Woman style. "Don't get mad. I don't want any of them to get in trouble, okay?"

Seeing her get all riled up and protective of his pack had Max falling in love with her all over again. He had to put on a mad face just to keep from smiling at her like a fool. "I'm not making that promise."

He'd promise her the moon or anything else she wanted.

"Fine." She wagged her finger at him. "But they came to me because they did what they needed to for love. You remember that."

Uh-oh. Why did he have a feeling love was going to come back to bite him on the ass?

SECRETS REVEALED

*G*al spotted the Grimm pack infiltrators at story time easily. The women and children they'd brought along had that look that only families living in a cycle of abuse showed. Outwardly, friendly and happy to be there. But to anyone who paid close attention, they were fearful of every little move and tried hard not to draw any attention to themselves.

The two men who were supposed to be fathers couldn't care less about what their kids were learning. They needed some lessons in espionage if you asked her. If they didn't want her to know they were there, maybe they should do something other than stare at her like hungry wolves.

Or maybe that was the point. They did want her intimidated.

Lucky for her four of the other families here for the evening reading of Brown Bear, Brown Bear and the subsequent animal masks craft were Troikas. At first Gal objected to bringing the kids. She didn't want them to get hurt. But one of the enforcers insisted his wife was a much better hand to hand combat fighter than he was. They also explained the contingency escape plan and assured her they all knew what to do in case of an emergency.

Here she was coloring a wolf mask with a giggling five-year old who clearly had the kind of crush on her that little boys got for their teachers, librarians, and babysitters.

"Wolfgang, let Ms. Shirvan help the other kids with their masks too," the little boys mother said and mouthed 'sorry' to her.

Gal stifled a laugh. Wolfgang and his family weren't even pack. There was no way she was naming her own children anything corny that had anything to do with wolves. Her stomach did a flip-flop thinking of a little boy like Wolfie running around with Max's blue eyes. She was silly thinking about kids already, but in her heart, she could hardly wait.

"Yes, Ms. Shirvan. Why don't you see how little Tammy is doing." One of the Grimm fakers motioned toward a little girl quietly coloring her own wolf mask in all black.

"I'd be happy to." Gal wanted to stick her tongue out at the man. Instead she held her face to show him she wasn't afraid and sat on the floor next to the little girl. She picked up the brightest blue crayon she could. The eye holes were cut out of the mask of course so the kids could see out, but she outlined the almond shape in Max's blue. She spoke softly to the child hoping she would understand Gal was a safe person. "Hello. My name's Galyna."

The girl scribbled hard across the face of the mask. "Tabby."

Her voice was barely more than a disgruntled whisper. "Sorry, honey, what was that?"

"My name is Tabby. Not Tammy. He always gets it wrong." She didn't look up, but stopped coloring for a moment.

Not even her father. A disgusting bitter taste pinged at the back of Gal's throat and her heart was grilled like a kebab. "I see. Well, I promise to remember it's Tabby. I don't think I've seen you at the library before."

The scribbling recommenced. "We don't get to do fun stuff since mama let him move into her room. I don't let him in mine though."

Gal made herself a silent promise to do everything in her power to stop these one-blood assfaces from terrorizing any other little girls. Even if she had to rip out their throats herself.

Geez. Where had that last bit come from? Some new blood-thirsty thoughts had been popping into her head since Max bit her. He did say he didn't know whether she was going to turn into a wolf or not. No one knew what happened when a wolf bit a human anymore. She and Key, the woman from the sheriff's department were the first in like a thousand years or something.

Key had developed some kind of psychic powers and creepy glowing eyes. Max suspected the witchy women Aleksei had encountered were also bitten humans. Gal gave herself a mental check. She concentrated really hard on the little girl's forehead to see if she could see the child's future or read her thoughts or something.

The girl looked up at her and wrinkled her nose. "Why are you staring at me like that?"

Busted. "Sorry. I was just admiring your hair. I can't get mine to make pretty waves like yours does. It's just always plain and straight."

The child examined her. "I'll trade you my curls if you let me have your pretty blue eyes."

Strange. Gal's eyes were brown, as were everyone else's in her family. "I don't think it works that way."

"Yeah. Mama says you can't fix pretty." The girl shrugged and went back to her dark coloring job.

Gal's emotions bubbled over for this young girl and her life. She prayed she could help. "I think my mother would say a mouse should eat you up. Which is my family's way of saying you're a very cute and clever girl, Tabby. I hope you can come back to the library soon."

The Grimm man squatted beside them and patted the girl on the head while staring at Galyna. "Oh, we'll be back. You can count on that."

Gal stared right back. "Good. I'll be waiting."

She hoped to diminish his enthusiasm for attacking her by convincing him he had very little to gain. Thanks to Sun Tzu she didn't give the guy a chance to react. She jumped up and clapped her hands to get everyone's attention. "Time to clean up, kids. Crayons in the box, but feel free to take home extra masks to color if you want."

As planned the Troika families dawdled and hung around to check out books. One of the mothers motioned her into the stacks under the guise of helping to find a book about dolphins. She lowered her voice to barely above a whisper. "None of us recognized either of those other wolves. They'll know we could scent them. But either they're doing a damn good job of hiding their emotions and intentions, or they have something masking them. I can't smell a thing besides that they are wolves."

Was that what she smelled tonight? That kind of warm

summer night after the rain scent that reminded her of Max. "It seems kind of risky for them to be so blatantly out in the open like that knowing other wolves could identify them."

"Agreed. My mate texted Max to let him know they are not hiding themselves. We all think they are trying to intimidate us. I have no doubt now that they'll show up tonight."

"Then the plan is working. Let's keep it going." Gal grabbed a book and raised her voice. "Here. I think your daughter will love this one. Lots of pictures of dolphins, orcas, and manatees."

That was phase one of the plan complete. Now to step two. After she finished packing up the story time kit, Gal stopped by the front desk where Sean, the library's assistant manager was sorting through a stack of books to be weeded from the collection. "Thanks for covering for me tonight, Sean. I really appreciate it."

"Not a problem. I'm happy to swap for next Saturday. Yummy rugby players are my jam."

Galyna had used her long-standing skills of taarof and maybe bribed him with tickets to the local rugby team's next game. "Cool. So I am off to Sleepy Folk then to get a drink."

That didn't sound weird or awkward. Nooooo.

Sean stuck his finger in his ear. "Uh, you don't have to yell. I'm right here."

Oops. Maybe she had said that a bit loud. "Sorry. Just excited for a Saturday night off, I guess. I'm just gonna go throw this on my desk. See you next week."

She trucked out the back door and found Heli waiting for her, right on time. She had her hands in her pockets and her cheery disposition was buried under ten feet of red teary eyes.

"You're totally buying me a drink for dragging me out tonight."

"Oh no, what happened? No one hurt you, did they?" Gal's skin tingled and she felt like she was going to burst out of her skin. If anyone had touched Heli, she was going to eat their faces off.

"I went to ask Kosta if he knew anything about Zara and he broke up with me. Well, I mean, we weren't official or anything in the first place, but he said he can't be seen with me anymore. It was awful. He wouldn't say why or anything. The rat. Now I'm sure he knows something about what's happened to Zara." She sniffled and rubbed her nose on her sleeve.

Well, crap. It had been hard enough to get Max to agree to let her bring Heli along tonight. Selena had been on her side, but wouldn't commit to saying that Heli and Kosta were true mates. But because she'd been there for the other attack and Zara was still MIA, he'd finally agreed that Heli needed to be under their protection.

But she'd been counting on Kosta. She knew he was still cranky about her and Max, but she knew he had feelings for Heli. He was a rat. A super rat. Hmm. Gal was going to have to work on that. She had a feeling Selena would help.

"I'll totally buy. I found out something about what's going on with the Troikas, and you're going to need a drink when you find out." She put her arm through Heli's and got them walking toward old town and Sleepy Folk.

Heli yanked them to a stop. "What do you know? They are in the mafia aren't they? Do they know where Zara is?"

"They aren't mafia." And what they were was going to blow her mind. "But it's big and I want to wait until we get to

Sleepy Folk because Max is a big part of this and he's going to want to talk to you."

"I don't like this. Just tell me."

Behind Heli's back Gal saw one of the Grimms also walking toward town. A weird smell like smoke after a candle was blown out wafted toward her. It was definitely coming from him too. "Umm. I'm going to tell you, but there's some kind of sketchy looking guy coming toward us and he's freaking me out. Can we hurry to the bar?"

Heli bunched her fists and narrowed her eyes. "Let's go before I do something stupid like go punch his lights out. I'm so fucking tired of men who think they can do shit to women."

Whoa. Heli was on fire. She really did need a drink. They hurried the three more blocks and were completely out of breath by the time they got into the pie shop.

"Who are those guys? When did Sleepy Folk get giant bouncers?"

Two of the men that Gal recognized as ones from the crew who'd approached her about their human girlfriends were stationed at either side of the stairwell that went down to the speakeasy part of the bar. They were turning a couple away. "Sorry. New ordinance by the city. We're at capacity and can't let anyone else in until someone comes out. But here are some coupons for a free slice of pie and a waved cover charge over at the Rogue Saloon and Emporium."

"Ah, man. I really wanted to try that new s'more martini here everyone is talking about,"the girl whined.

"Yeah, babe. But, free pie. Come on." The other young woman pulled her girlfriend toward the pie counter.

Heli frowned and folded her arms. "Looks like we're not going to get in."

Gal dragged her over anyway. The bouncers were for show so that only wolves and their families got in tonight. "I've got a connection."

The guys waved them through right away and halfway down the stairs, Gal stopped. "Heli. You're going to hear some weird stuff tonight. I want you to know before we go in there, that it's all totally legit. We're counting on you to not freak out, and to keep everything you see and hear a secret."

"Oh-kay. You're scaring me a little bit. Does this have anything to do with Zara?" Panic was building behind Heli's eyes and tears were threatening to fall again.

Gal grabbed Heli into a hug and held her tight. "I don't know for sure, but we think it does. So that means it's even more important that you get on board with everything as fast as you possibly can. It's going to be a lot to process, but I promise, everything is going to be okay."

"You can't promise that." Heli sniffled and seemed so, so tired. "She could already be dead and I went back to the Sheriff's department today and they still won't do anything. There's something weird going on there too."

Maybe this wasn't a good idea. Gal had to believe that they were doing the right thing by bringing Heli into the loop. It sure would help if Kosta wasn't being a rat at the moment. "You're right. I can't promise that Zara is going to be okay. But I can swear to you that Max and I are going to do everything we can to find her and bring her home safe."

Heli pushed away and narrowed her eyes at Gal. "Why is everything all you and Max all of a sudden? You've been dating the guy for like a week."

Harley came up the steps and motioned for them to come down. "Galyna? Can you follow me? We're getting ready to start."

"Ready?" Gal asked. When Heli nodded, they went down into the bar and found Heli a seat at the counter.

Gal didn't miss the looks they were both getting from everyone else gathered there. Only a few insiders already knew about Max becoming the alpha and claiming her. The rest either gave her wary looks or grumbled to their neighbors. "I'll be right back. I just need to find Max. Don't go anywhere."

Heli nodded and said something to Harley as Gal walked away. The last thing she saw was the three shot glasses Harley set down in front of her.

Gal paced back and forth in the little hallway between the bar and the storeroom at the back of Sleepy Folk. As far as she knew, she and Heli were the only humans here at the moment. But more were on the way. She was the welcoming committee for when the other men and women were snuck in the back way.

Harley had nearly kissed her when she'd told him the plan. Having big, growly Max with his arm around her shoulder and his snarl on had put an end to that.

Max was still wary about bringing other humans into the pack meeting. She'd gotten him to concede that their mating was going to seem a heck of a lot more legitimate if he wasn't the only one who was allowed to break the rules. All she could do now was pray that the other wolves who were involved with humans had chosen wisely.

Selena reassured them both that there were a lot more fated mates out there than any of them suspected. She'd told them she couldn't imagine that a true mate would ever willingly betray their loved one. She still hadn't yet mentioned how she knew who anyone's true mates were, only that she did.

The back door, which was an old school cellar, opened and a group of eight people made their way down. Gal recognized four of the six women, because they were all around her age. But there were older ones. One woman was maybe in her forties and the other at least fifties. She only knew one of the two men that joined them. She greeted each of them quietly with a wave until Harley had the door shut again.

He gave one of the girls a peck on the cheek and then scurried back to the bar. The rest was up to Gal.

"Hi. I'm Galyna. Max is my...wolf." It felt strange to say mate to a group of other humans. She indicated to each of the others to introduce themselves and who they were attached to. When everyone was finished the group looked around at each other, most visibly relieved. She supposed because they weren't alone in their secrets anymore.

One of the girls Gal recognized from high school asked the question that was probably on most of their minds. "Are we sure this is the right thing to do. Bastion said we could be ostracized from the community, or even killed if anyone found out he'd revealed himself to me."

The eldest of the group stepped forward. "Do you love him honey, with all your heart? Do you feel like he's the only one for you so deep down that even thinking about him being with someone else feels like your soul would be ripped out?"

The young lady nodded.

"Then this is the right thing. The truth is always the best choice. I've been keeping this secret for twenty-five years and

I'm damn sure glad to know I'm not the only one. I'll bet there are more of us and the pack are just afraid to let it be known."

The other woman Gal didn't know spoke too. "I've been waiting since the first Troika boy was born to see if he could change the world. I never liked that we had to keep our love to ourselves. No wedding, no kids. I've been praying for this."

Wow. Gal never would have suspected how hard being in love with a person and not being able to tell the whole world about the wishes left on their hearts. It had been hard enough for her for one afternoon. Hearing these women's stories and seeing the look on the rest of the groups faces confirmed for her that they were making the right call.

"Max has warned me this won't be a walk in the park. There will be wolves who don't like the idea of changing the status quo." In fact he'd warned her it could be even worse than that. He expected a fight and had assigned all the enforcers who had a human here tonight, plus a few extras to guard them all. "So be prepared for that. Also know that I have your back and so does Max. This won't be easy, change never is. But I believe in my heart, it's going to make the pack stronger and all of your lives and the lives of your loved ones better to come out of the shadows."

The taller of the two men smiled at her. "Jace said you were a good match for Max. Lead on miss librarian. This can't be any harder than coming out to my parents over the Christmas turkey. If I can do that I can tell a bunch of stuffy old fart wolves where to shove their one-blood ideologies."

The hardest thing Gal had done before this was tell her parents she was moving and out and no, she didn't need any more pickles for her fridge at Heli and Zara's. She hoped she had half the strength of these incredible people standing in front of her now.

Max stuck his head into the hallway. "Showtime, *detka*."

Gal rubbed her arms, that same feeling she'd had at the library of coming out of her skin prickled all up and down her limbs. Her eyesight suddenly went sharper and she could smell a thousand distinct scents and hear every little movement of the bodies around her. Max rushed to her side and grabbed her face in his hands.

"Galyna, your eyes. They're shining with the light of a wolftress."

She had only one thing she could say to that. "Grrr-ruff."

CALL TO ARMS

*M*oon in the sky, Galyna's wolf was coming out to play. Max's own wolf responded like a puppy on crack. It wanted to run and jump and lick her face and howl at the moon with her. This could solve everything. If the mate bite did turn humans into wolf-shifters than there would be way less resistance to accepting them into the pack.

One of the other women standing in the hallway gasped. "Oh, she got the wolf. Lucky girl. I wish I had. I'd give anything to run with Harley as a wolf."

Several others nodded, but a tall guy and an older woman both looked surprised. The woman glanced around at the others. "You don't shift?"

Three of the women and one man shook their heads no. The young man raised his hand. "After Olga and I mated, I started seeing things. I thought they were ghosts or something, or that I'd gone crazy. Then this one time, she saw them too. We tested it a bit and figured out I can conjure up what we call echoes. It's easier if I show you."

He closed his eyes, took a deep breath and held one hand out into the hallway. A ghost-like version of Gal floated into the hall and leaned against the wall, watching the back door expectantly.

"Holy crap. That's me, but like fifteen minutes ago." Gal reached out to touch the partially translucent image and it disappeared like steam dissipating.

One of the other women spoke up. "I can tell if someone is telling the truth or lying. It's why I agreed to come tonight."

"I can do this." A woman who looked around forty pointed to each of them and one by one in turn, they each suddenly looked like some movie star or other celebrity. Gal made a very sexy Marilyn Monroe. She let them all stare at each other for a moment and then snapped her fingers. Everyone went back to looking like themselves. "It's only a glamour, something seen, but it's not a real change."

Gal held up her hands. "Let me get this straight in my mind. Some of you can shift and some of you have some kind of, for lack of a better term, magical or psychic abilities. Is it something inherent or does it have to do with being around the wolves? What's the cause?"

A voice came from behind them. "The mate's bite."

Max turned, surprised by his mother. "Mom. Why do I have the feeling you know a whole hell of a lot more about all of this than you've told me? What do you know about all of this?"

Selena sighed and approached the group. "I've been keeping tabs on each of you from the second your wolf found you. I may have even given a few pack members a shove in your direction."

His mother's matchmaking had gone a little too far this time. She'd willingly helped at least eight wolves break wolf law. Nine if he counted himself. "What? You had to know this would create chaos in the pack, in all of wolf society."

"Yes, and it's damn well time we got a shake-up." Her normally calm and collected demeanor slipped away and a fervor injected her voice. "The Volkov's were no longer working for the best interest of our people. They were corrupt. All except for Mikhail. Your brother went to Russia to help him escape the machinations of the old world. He was going to come here and bring wolfkind into the twenty-first century. We haven't been hunted in hundreds of years for god's sake. It's time we quit hiding."

Well, fuck him. Max's mother was a revolutionary. "If Niko was in on all of this, why would he kill Mikhail?"

Selena grabbed him by the shoulder. "Use your head, son. He died trying to save the Tzar. Niko believed in this cause with his whole heart. He thought Mik was the best chance we had. With his word as law, we could all finally be free to find our true mates no matter if they are wolf, human, or fricking unicorns. We all deserve that, and you out of anyone should understand. You've got your true mate."

He did, in large part because of her. She'd been keeping secrets from them all for years. "Did dad...know?"

"Your father liked the old ways." She tipped her head to the side and frowned. "He couldn't believe the Volkov's were corrupt. His family helped put them in power and he was blindly loyal to them."

So that was a no. Max didn't like being in the dark and he doubted anyone else in his pack did either. If they were going to be the start of this revolution he needed to get them all on his side. They couldn't do that by hiding. God, he hoped they didn't all end up with their heads chopped off.

Harley stuck his head into the hallway. "Hey, boss. The troops are getting antsy. We ready to get this show on the road?"

Not even close. "Yeah. Get everyone quieted down. I'll be there in a minute."

He needed a new plan and quick. He'd hoped tonight was simply taking his claim to be alpha and introducing his mate. The only complication was supposed to be that she was human. He hadn't decided yet if he was going to announce that the ban on mating humans was lifted, in their pack at least. Only if he'd been pressed.

That wasn't the way a strong alpha led his pack.

Time to wolf up.

"Everyone stay here until I call for you. I am going to ask you all to reveal yourselves and your relationships. I can't promise that you won't get hurt, but I will do everything in my power to protect you. If you can't do this, or aren't ready, say so now and I'll call your wolves to escort you home." He looked each of the mates in the eye and not a one of them backed down. They each had more guts than he did in their own way. Good. They were going to need them.

"I know there are infiltrators from the packs we are at war with in the crowd, and they may use this as their excuse to strike. Be careful. The enforcers are ready for them and will take them down, so don't get in their way." He stopped and stared for a moment at the ones who had shown their powers. "On second thought, if you can help by using your abilities, do. We're going to need all the help we can get."

The group all nodded and looked ready to go out and kick

some ass. Max took Galyna's hand. "Ready?"

"As I'll ever be." She stood up on her tippy-toes and gave him a quick kiss. "For luck."

He led her to the end of the hall and with a squeeze of her hand left her there until he was ready to present her to the pack. Max took a fortifying breath and stepped up onto the small stage to face his pack. The room fell silent almost immediately. Wolves he'd known his entire life filled the room. They'd look to him and his family to keep them safe, secure, and protected. Tonight he would ask them to give up some of that security and fight for their futures.

Max cleared his throat and addressed the room with the power of the alpha in his voice. "Thank you all for coming on such short notice and during volatile times. I wouldn't have asked you if this wasn't important. My father led this pack with loyalty and dignity and it is with a sad heart I tell you that Piotr Illyvich Troika has been killed by the dishonorable packs of Grimm and Crescent. They come to claim our pack."

The room erupted into boos and hisses. Most of them already knew. It didn't take long for news like this to spread through a pack. He let them grumble for a moment and then continued. "I claim this pack as my own, from this night forward, I Maxsim Aleksandr Piotryvich Troika am your alpha. If any wish to challenge me, do so now."

Max waited an entire count of a hundred before he nodded his head acknowledging there were no challengers. Someone in the back of the room beat out a rhythm on their table with a mug or a hand and chanted, "Troika, Troika, Troika."

Soon almost the entire room joined in until the bar was filled with the sound of a rallying pack. He let them build themselves up into a frenzy of pack loyalty and fervor. He hoped they would have the same enthusiasm for the battles ahead. A wolf from the front row handed him a mug of beer and he held it over his head, toasting the crowd. In a few long swallows he drained the drink and slammed the glass down to the floor, shattering it in celebration. Dozens of others followed suit and soon the floor was littered with shards of glass.

Max held his hand up and quieted the crowd back down. "We can not allow these other packs to invade Rogue and create havoc in our land. They have declared war on us without honor. I will not stand for that. I call upon you to join me in battling our enemies until we are victorious."

Almost every man in the room stood to volunteer and surprisingly a few women as well. They joined their voices in a haunting howl that would scare any foe. Maybe his pack was already far more progressive than he knew. Most wolves loved a good fight so rallying the troops was easy. Now for the hard part.

"I need you all to understand that with this war, we will have many enemies. Not simply the Grimms, Crescent, and the Bay, but wolves around the world are disturbed by the Troika involvement with the Volkovs and the death of the Tzar." The room went decidedly darker at the mention of what most of them probably felt was their first son's shame. It was time for them to know the truth.

"We won't be able to convince them all, but I want each and every one of you to know that my brother, Nikolai,"

Max's voice choked on the emotions he'd suppressed since the news of Niko's death. "Niko did not kill Tzar Mikhail Volkov. He died trying to save him from schemes of his corrupt family."

The people in the room were as shocked as Max had been at this news. He struck them all with more revelations. "Mikhail had great plans for our world. He above all wanted better for each of us and planned for sweeping changes that would affect our lives. In doing so, he gave us the secret weapon that will help us not only defeat our enemies, but allow our society to evolve. For too long we have lived oppressed. For hundreds of years our laws stated that we must hide ourselves from the world and that law denied us the ability to find our true mates."

Someone shouted from the crowd. "Some wolves find their true mate. I did."

"Yes, some have. Some were lucky that their true mates were other wolves. Most are not so fortunate. I believe that finding the mate that is right for you, the one who is made especially for you and you for them doesn't have to be a one in a million chance as we've all been led to believe. Mikhail didn't think so either. According to my sources, he was about to declare that wolfkind would no longer be required to mate only among other wolves, that we could all go out in search of our true mates no matter if they were wolf or not."

This time the crowd did not remain silent in their shock. Many spoke at once.

"You're suggesting that we treat the humans, other shifters, elves, fairies, and so on as any other person we might mate? What about the mate's bite?"

"We can't bite a human. That's disgusting."

"No one even knows what will happen to a human who is bit by a wolf. They might die."

Harley couldn't hold his tongue and blurted out. "They won't die."

"How do you know?" All eyes turned on Harley and he in turn stared up at Max.

Max held out his hand toward Galyna and motioned her to join him on the stage. She took a deep breath and stepped up next to him and took his hand. Murmurs rippled through those gathered and not all of them were friendly. So it began. "I present to you, Galyna Shirvan, my true mate."

Gal pulled her collar away to reveal the tattoo on her neck and shoulder.

"You're telling me, this fat bitch is supposed to be our matriarch?"

Max growled, his fangs and claws extended, and his eyes glowed with his wolf's anger. Gal put a hand on his arm to stop him from attacking the dickpotato that had resorted to calling her names. "It's okay. He's scared and upset. They're only words."

Another man swooped out of the shadows in the corner of the bar and threw the man against the wall, pinning him there with a hand that was more wolf than human. He snarled, dark and low. "That's your alpha's mate, asshole. Be careful how you talk about her."

Kosta. Her defender was the last man Max expected to stand up for her in light of his earlier tantrum.

The man scratched at Kosta, trying to get away. His own wolf was rising up as indicated by the sprouts of hair on his hands and arms. "You can't expect me to accept his fat fetish as my matriarch. She isn't even a wolftress."

Kosta slammed the man against the wall again, hard enough that a spray of debris fell from the ceiling. "You can calmly and intelligently argue wolf law and how Galyna's position will have repercussions on all of our society, ass-munch. But her body, every luscious curve of it is no one's business but hers and her mate's. Got it?"

If it was a wolftress they wanted, that's what they would get. Max turned Gal to face him. "Galyna listen to me. This is going to hurt, but it won't be for long, I promise. Just keep your eyes on me and listen to my voice."

"Max? What... oh no. We don't even know if I can. So far all I've been able to do is have some sparkly wolf eyes."

"You can, and you will." Max let his own wolf rise up enough that the alpha voice, the one that no member of his pack could deny pooled in his mouth. "Change, Galyna Shir-van. Let your wolf out. Show your wolftress to everyone here."

Gal closed her eyes and her face contorted as the pain of her first shift hit her. She gripped his hands so hard he thought they might break. It was a pain he would happily endure for her. Her own bones cracked and her skin split. Gal screamed out but her voice quickly turned from a human woman to the howl of a wolf.

The clothes she'd worn split from her body and dropped in shreds to the floor as her claws, teeth, and fur pushed out taking on the form of the wolf. Before his eyes, Max's beau-tiful mate became his beautiful wolf. She was a dark choco-latey brown, save a grey circle on her right front shoulder. An anomaly in her fur the shape of a silvery moon.

A wolf darted forward through the crowd and jumped through the air straight at Galyna. He was not a Troika, but one of the Grimms who Max and his enforcers had allowed to sneak in. Max's own wolf burst forth to protect his mate and he met the bastard straight on, colliding in the air.

Too late he realized this wolf was a pawn and the real attack came from behind where Gal was open and exposed.

The world around Galyna was technicolored and loud. She could see things like body heat, and she knew immediately who was human, who was wolf, and who was something in between. It was all very distracting. She couldn't seem to keep her mind focused on just one thing.

Max. If she could concentrate on him, she would be okay. She stared at him wondering how she hadn't ever recognized the soul of the wolf wavering around him. Then suddenly, the wolf was more than a mirror image of Max, he was Max.

Oh. Max had shifted into his wolf form too and he was jumping into the air. Another wolf crashed into him and they dropped to the floor in a flurry of snarls and fur.

Gal shook her head, knowing she should help him. She couldn't quite seem to get her feet to work. She had too many of them and not enough hands. One step forward and she plopped down on her butt. She felt like a newborn giraffe, trying to get up and walk for the first time.

Galyna, run. Max's voice popped into her head. He

sounded scared. She'd never heard him even a little worried before.

She opened her mouth to tell him that she couldn't and a weird wroo-wroo-wroo sound came out. Crap. That wasn't right. Think. Think. How did Max talk to her.

In her head. She opened her mind and reached out with her thoughts. *I. Don't. Can't. How?*

She sure thought mental telepathy would be easier. Becoming a wolf meant she was learning how to walk and talk all over again.

Gal was smart, dammit. She had an advanced degree. She could figure out how to move her feet. Her butt went up in the air and her tail wagged. Which felt super weird, but also happy. Okay, good. Now one foot, now a back foot. Good. Now the other foot, and the other back foot.

She wasn't going to get far like this. *Max. I'm. Help. You. Coming. To.*

At least those were words in a sentence, even if they did come out stunted and not quite the right order. Hey, if people could figure out what Yoda was saying, her mate could probably figure out what she meant. Now to find him. More and more wolves were joining in the fight and she'd lost track of Max. *Where? Are you?*

No. Get away, Gal. Run.

Just like a man to not accept help. She knew kung-fu for goodness sake. She could take care of herself. *No way. Jose.*

Ooh. That was an actual sentence. She was getting better at this. A few more minutes and she'd be running circles around these clowns to the left of her, and jokers to the right that were trying to take on her pack.

Galyna Shirvan. Change. Shift back into your human form and run. There was a different tone to Max's voice that time and it made her wolf want to whimper.

Her body stretched until she was sure she was going to break. Then she did. Her wolf howled and in the next second it was her own voice screaming. She was human again standing among a gauntlet of snapping jaws and teeth naked as a jay-walking-bird. Her feet were moving of their own accord and without a single signal from her own mind, she was running.

Gal grabbed a discarded oversized t-shirt from a table as she scooted by and threw it on over her head. She couldn't even stop running long enough to see whose it might have been. Dog gone it. What kind of spell had Max put on her that she had to do exactly what he said. Fine, two could play at this game. She would run, but he hadn't said where to go.

She pointed her feet in the direction of the back hallway where the rest of the human mates were waiting. The whole lot of them looked frightened and several of them were huddled together. "Galyna. Thank God. What's going on out there? It sounds awful."

"No time to explain except that the Grimms and probably some other baddies have picked a fight. We knew they would. Time to show the pack why having humans on our team is going to rock." The plan was forming in her mind as she spoke. Good ole Sun Tzu came to mind one more time. "All warfare is based on deception. We're going to fool the bad guys and scare their pants off so they never want to mess with us again. Okay?"

They group nodded. "Great. If you can shift into a wolf, I want you to do that in a minute right at the entrance where they'll be able to see you. Then you, sorry I didn't learn your name, dude who can make echoes. Put that echo on repeat so it looks like hundreds of wolves are pouring out of the hall and into the room. Got it?"

Dude nodded. "No problem."

"Good. Jenny, use your glamour on all of us so we look like the biggest scariest wolves you've ever seen. Go Hollywood werewolves. They haven't seen anyone but me shift, so let's make them think we're rabid monsters, huh?"

"I can do that."

"What about us?" The truth-teller and two others who Gal hadn't found out what their powers were stood together.

"Umm, I'm thinking on my feet here and I'm not sure. But you get the game. Make them think our normal force is extraordinary and that they should flee the heck out of here. Go with your guts."

There was no more time and Gal was getting tired of jogging in place. "Now let's go save our mates."

Team human mates went into action. Gal and the other two wolf shifters bounded out of the hallway and were followed by the echoes a thousand times over. More wolves had joined the fray including a huge poop-brown wolf she didn't recognize. His muzzle was already covered in blood and he was facing off against Max.

Except it wasn't a fair fight. Not even a little bit. Max was limping and she could see a huge gash in his back leg. His back was up against a wall, and he was protecting a black wolf lying on the ground, its head cradled in the lap of Heli.

Crap. It was Kosta. He wasn't dead. Gal could see his chest rising and falling. But he also wasn't moving in any other way. Heli had tears spilling down her face. She crooned to

Kosta and caressed his muzzle. Her hands were covered in blood.

Gal prayed that her glamour was in place and that she looked scary as hell. Because she was about to get in between two snarling wolves and try to save someone's life. Her someone.

She put her best monster growly face on and ran toward Max and the poop-colored wolf. "I'm coming to get you, shithead. Run away now or prepare to be flushed down into the sewer where you belong."

Max growled at her. *I thought I told you to run.*

"I am running. You didn't say where. Shush your face now and let me save your butt." Gal raised her arms over her head and walked like Frankenstein's Monster toward them, groaning and moaning. Any second now he was going to run away whimpering.

The poop wolf growled at them both. *Good try, little mate.*

Little mate. This was one of the guys who'd been at her house. She bet all the tea on a slow boat from China that he knew where Zara was.

I have my own witch who showed me exactly how this would all go down. Your glamour does nothing for you. I already know I'm going to defeat your alpha and take over this poor excuse for a pack. You might as well submit to me now. Every word out of this wolf's mind was laced with a creepy confidence.

"I'll make you a deal, shit-for-fur. How about you submit to me instead, tell me where Zara is, and then roll over and die. How does that sound?"

I am going to enjoy teaching you exactly what you can do with that smart mouth of yours. I guarantee it won't be used for talking back to me ever again. Not after I shove my coc--

Max erupted, charging toward the brown wolf, going directly for his throat. The dumbass had been distracted by Gal and had exposed himself to Max's fury. A centimeter before his jaws closed around the bastard's throat two other wolves shot toward him, one from each side and took him down to the ground in a tangle of claws and teeth and fur.

Galyna gasped and rushed forward, but the asshole wolf shifted and grabbed her, holding her to his chest, encircling her throat. She scratched and clawed at him, her own wolf rising up, but she couldn't quite get the shift to come on. "Come on, Max. Get them, get them."

Max kicked one of the attackers hard enough that it went flying across the stage, but the other one used that as its opportunity to redouble its attack. It jumped toward Max and chomped down on the side of his head. Gal heard the bones crunch and Max's body went limp.

Noooooooooooooooooooooo.

Something inside of Galyna's chest broke, as painfully as if her heart had been ripped from between her ribs. She screeched and bit down on the arm holding her. Her mouth twisted and reshaped itself into that of her wolf's deadly jaw. She snapped down on the man's flesh hard, reveling in the snap of bone in her mouth.

He wailed and jumped back from her, then shifted into his own shitty wolf again. He growled low and circled her, preparing for the ultimate showdown.

Galyna's wolf had had enough. It burst out of her skin and this time she didn't even acknowledge the pain. It was nothing compared to the pounding anguish in her heart and soul. If Max was dead, no one else was going to live. Not while Galyna could avenge him.

These bastards were going down. The wolftress who'd been flailing around inside of Galyna was in control now, all limbs, muscles, and anger working just fine now that she gave herself over to the beast fully. She was one blood-thirsty bitch. Anyone who tried to destroy her pack, her mate, her new found badass life was going to be very, very sorry. And she was going to have a lot of fun doing it.

I am woman hear me roar.

I am your alpha now, little mate. You must do as I say. The same power Max had rolled through the wolf's voice in her head, but it had no effect on her. She shook her head and wagged her tail at him.

You'll never be my alpha or anyone else's, asshole. You don't deserve to have power over anyone. She lunged at the Grimm's alpha.

He dodged her and snapped his jaw at her barely missing her shoulder. Asshole had tried to bite her mark. The one thing of Max she had left.

Try that again, you piece of shit. Let's see who is going to submit to whom. She knew she was goading him and didn't give him a chance to actually reply. She ran forward, jumped into the air and landed on his back. In one giant snarling bite, she ripped his throat out, decapitated him, and spit the bloody head to the floor.

Gross. The asshole tasted like asshole.

Galyna howled and opened her mind, reaching for Max, knowing he wasn't there. *I have avenged you, my love. The Grimm alpha is dead at my hands. I swear to you I will do everything I can to protect this pack and carry on your legacy.*

A faint whisper of a voice returned to her. *Declare your claim on his pack.*

Max? Her heart sang with joy. She ran to him and did the only thing she could think of. She licked his face.

Thank you, love. I'll be okay. My wolf needs a little time to heal. Go on now. You have defeated an alpha. His pack is now yours if you claim it. Do it now and end the war before it starts.

She would fly to the moon and back if Max asked her to. She jumped up on the nearest table and howled, getting everyone's attention. *I claim the Grimm pack for myself and for my mate. The one-blood's will terrorize the people and wolves of Rogue no more. Stop your battle for you are all now one under my banner.*

That should do it. She sounded all Game of Thrones and stuff. The last remaining wolves who were fighting stopped at her declaration.

Max's voice popped into her head once more. *Command them to bow at your feet and declare their fealty to you.*

Really? That doesn't seem very progressive.

It's what they understand.

Okay. She lifted her voice again. *Bow to me and show your fealty, but if you are ready to join this revolution, lift your faces to the moon and declare it to be so.*

The wolves in the room bowed one by one, except for a few who scrambled away. She let them go. They would live to fight another day because Gal understood this battle was only beginning.

She was the first to lift her head and howl at the moon, but soon they all were declaring themselves to her and their fight for freedom to choose their own mates. Declaring they would be a part of the revolution of true mates, of true love.

Rock on.

Key, who'd been sitting calmly near the small raised stage

the whole time stood and greeted Galyna as a wolf. She reached her hand out and touched Gal's head, scratching behind her ears as if she was nothing more than a puppy. It felt great and she'd remember that for next time Max was in wolf form and she was not.

"I lied to him. He thought he would win. I didn't want him to. He was a dick." Key turned and glanced toward the steps leading down to the speakeasy. "A dragon, a witch, and wolf walk into a bar."

A big man who looked a lot like an extra hot Jason Momoa with a prosthetic arm, and a super beautiful woman dressed all in white floated down the steps.

"I told you we were gonna miss the good part, but you wanted to stop for ice cream," the woman said.

"Sorry, my love. But you know I can't resist rainbow sherbet with rainbow sprinkles on top." He lifted a chocolate dipped cone and gave it a slurp. "Besides, I'm practicing for later."

He waggled his eyebrows and flicked his tongue in a very naughty way around the tip of the ice cream.

The woman rolled her eyes, but smiled. "Stop flirting with me. We have to find our... oh there she is. Kur, darling, can you heal the wolves real quick. He's going to want to be conscious for this."

The man crossed the room, took another lick of his ice cream cone and blew a soft green mist over Max and Kosta. Both men shifted back into their human forms and not only were their wounds gone, neither had a scar, blemish, or even a freckle in sight. "Oops. A little to much Dragon's Breath. Sorry."

Galyna's wolf pulled itself back inside of her and she

shifted into her human self again. She plopped down onto the floor where Max lay, wide-eyed and blinking. She touched his face and he grabbed her hand, holding it tight and pressing her palm to his lips.

"You two can do all the kissing and baby-making later." The woman snapped her fingers and she and Max were both fully clothed and sitting at the bar. They were also the only ones here, aside from the man and woman.

Gal looked around and then back at the woman. "Where did everyone go?"

The woman shrugged and wandered behind the bar. She riffled around the bottles until she found what she was looking for. "It's late. I sent them all to their beds. Don't worry, they won't remember a thing. You two won't either."

She mixed a drink and pushed one in front of Gal and another in front of Max. "That should get your libidos going. You're going to have very beautiful and important children, you two are."

Max frowned. "Who are you?"

The woman laughed and touched her hand to her forehead. "Oh, goodness. Such poor manners I have. I'm--"

Galyna blinked and she and Max were back at Troika's house sitting in the living room. Kosta and Heli were there, and Selena. Sitting across from them, half hidden in the dark was another man.

He didn't move and Gal wasn't entirely sure he was alive. She tugged on Max's shirt-sleeve. "Max, who is that?"

Max stared at the man and breathed fast, but shallow. He swallowed three or four times without answering. Then he stood and crossed to the shadowy figure. "I am Maxsim Piotryvich Troika, alpha of the Troika pack of Rogue, New

York. This is my mate, Galyna Shirvan, alpha of the Grimm pack. Who are you and what are you doing in our home?"

The man stood and Galyna gasped. This changed everything. He spoke in a quiet and broken voice that hitched and cracked on the words. "I'm your big brother, Maxy. It's me, Niko."

TO THE MOON AND BACK

*E*ven though the moon was full in the sky, cloud cover was keeping the sacred circle in the Reserve from being totally lit up by its rays. That didn't matter to Max. Very little could make this night even more perfect. Tonight was the night when he and Gal would be mated and she would become the matriarch of his pack.

Yes, there were complications. She was also officially the alpha of the Grimms which was unprecedented. No woman had ever been an alpha before. She was bringing more changes than they were all ready for. But it was time. His mother had practically stood on the roof to shout girl power slogans to the world. Turned out she wasn't only a revolutionary, she was a good old-fashioned feminist too.

Then there was Niko.

He hadn't wanted to come tonight, but their mother had convinced him that if he truly was giving up his claim to be alpha of the Troikas like he insisted that he needed to witness the mating of the heir apparent and the soon to be matriarch.

The rest of the pack would have a hard enough time with him giving up his right to the title now that he was back.

Niko wasn't really back. His body was. His mind and soul were not. The depth of pain in Niko's eyes hurt Max's heart. He hoped that he and Gal would be able to help him heal.

None of them really understood how he'd come back to them. He'd told a strange tale of being pulled out of hell by a dragon, but that's all he would say for now. Max wouldn't pressure him. Niko would talk when he was ready. Until then, the family would take care of him. He'd done so much for all of them, that it was his turn to rest.

Max glanced up at the sky. The moon would reach its pinnacle soon. Where were his mother and Galyna?

There were other wolves around the circle that looked as anxious as he felt. They were all preparing to be officially mated tonight. Gal wasn't the only one who'd been invited to join this previously wolf only ritual. Six other women and two young men who were as in love with a wolf-shifter as Gal was with him stood dotted around the circle too.

There were a few other wolves looking for mates here too. Some still hoped that they would find a mate among their own kind. He hoped some of them did.

A soft breeze brought the scent of ripe peaches, berries, and the clean smell of moonlight to his nose. Max's wolf went on high alert, pushing all of his senses out, searching. Every cell in his body became ultra-awake, rejuvenated. His mate was near.

A light, beautiful and bright, coming through the forest caught his eye. The clouds over the moon parted and Galyna stepped into the clearing, the sacred circle illuminated in her presence. She glowed, literally shining as bright as the moon. She took his breath away, never to be returned.

Selena stepped up next to him and whispered in his ear. "I told you that you'd know when you'd found your true mate."

"She's beautiful, mom. How will everyone else not be jealous?" A sensation like his ribs squeezing him too tight, barreled through his chest. No one could tempt his mate away from him, and still he felt pangs of jealousy that anyone else should even look upon her.

"Because she only glows for you. Only true mates glow under the full moon to each other. Look around, the other lovers here all have that same awestruck look on their faces as you do, but they only have eyes for their own mates. Only they can see how their one and only lights up the night." Selena glanced at the other side of the circle, lingered for a moment and then gave Max a shove. "Go on. She's nervous waiting there for you. Go claim your mate, *sinochek*."

His Galyna. The most amazing woman he'd ever met. His true mate. Thank God for his meddling revolutionary mother or he might never have acted on the feelings he had for Gal. Their worlds were going to change, and not always for the better. The upheaval of their way of life had started even before Mikhail had been killed. Rules and laws held for centuries no longer applied, and wolves around the globe were looking to him and the Troikas for their next moves. Some in hope, and more with contempt, loathing, and disdain. The battle with the Grimms was only the beginning.

Tonight wasn't about the turmoil and war. Yes, he was making a loud statement that would be heard by every wolf-shifter alive today. Together, he and Gal were declaring the right to love each other.

No one had the right to control who he or any other wolf, human, dragon, witch, fairy, sprite, or any other being in the universe loved and wanted to be with.

Love is love.

Max loved Galyna. Always and forever, to the moon and back.

Wolf culture was changing, but the mating ceremony was one part of wolf life he looked forward to preserving. Everything else in their world could be upended. They needed comfort in one small but important custom being the same. Besides, he couldn't wait to touch, taste, and tantalize Gal until she was begging to be fucked.

Marked.

Claimed.

Mated.

In front of the rest of the pack, in front of all the other couples who were being mated tonight too. There was no more hiding, by anyone, who they loved. The age of oppression ended tonight. Right now.

Max walked to the center of the clearing and took Galyna's hand. Her touch gave him a jolt that sent tingles of achy pleasure to his heart, down his spine and pooled between his legs. While he was naked, she'd insisted on some clothing. She stood barefoot but wore a wispy white dress that offset her lovely olive skin beautifully. He could see her nipples and the dark thatch between her legs through the material. Flowers dotted her long dark hair like a halo. His angel, his goddess of love. She was absolutely divine. He wanted to eat her up.

Gal smiled up at him and then around the circle like she was seeing all the rest of the wolves and people for the first time. She shuffled her feet, and stared down at them, her breathing a bit faster than before. Everyone waited for him to start the ceremony.

He would, just as soon as his mate was ready. Max grabbed her around the waist, pressing his hand to the small of her back. "It's just you and me, *kriska.*"

She didn't look up and licked her lips. "The pack--"

"Shh. Look at me, only me." He caught her chin with his knuckles and gently raised her face to him. "This is about us, our love, our commitment to each other. They'll watch, and I'll bet a lot of them will even be turned on. How could they not be, with your pure, raw sensuality. They don't matter, Galyna. This moment isn't for them. Only you... and... me. Understand?"

Her eyes were dark with lust, but still guarded. "But--"

He cupped her glowing cheek in his hand. "No buts. I'm going to take your body under the full moon and stars. You are mine and I want everyone to know."

"Maxsim. Stop interrupting me, damn it." She waited a few seconds to make sure he wasn't going to stop her from saying it this time. "Two things. You're naked and you're glowing."

Her eyes darted around and he could practically hear her mind wondering if everyone was staring at them. Max pushed a hand into her hair and forced her eyes back to him. "You are glowing too. God, you're beautiful. The rest of them can't see this. Apparently fated mates only glow in the moonlight for each other. For the rest of them, their true mates are the ones lighting up the night and their souls."

The tension fell off of her then and she took a long relaxing breath. "I love that, Max. It's our telepathy of the heart manifested."

Telepathy of the heart. Yes, that described perfectly how

his heart was sure hers was the right one for him. Glowing or not, Galyna was his. Max kissed her, gently at first, taking his time to relish every touch and taste of her. When she was wanting and needy for more, he lifted his head to the sky and howled to the moon thanking it for bringing her into his life. A chorus of other howls, some wolf, and some human joined him.

The mating ceremony had officially begun. Wolves and human approached each other all around them, and broke off into couples. The sounds and smells of arousal, sex, mating, and pure fucking filled the night air. Max only had eyes for his mate.

"I love you Galyna. I have for longer than I can remember and I wish I had been strong enough to act on it before." His gaze was drawn to her lips and he couldn't help rubbing his thumb over them.

Gal sucked his thumb into her mouth and tickled the end with her tongue. She'd lost her reticence and joined in the play. "Don't regret our past. Now was the right time for us to find each other."

"I thank the moon every night for bringing us together. Are you ready to show everyone our love?" His body was more than ready, but he would wait if she needed more time. Although, he was going to tease and build up her anticipation higher the longer she waited.

Her eyes sparkled with mischief and love. "Yep. Let's make babies."

Max's heart and chest expanded, and he could feel every beat of his heart. He wanted to have lots and lots of kids with her. He wanted to rub his hands over her belly, big and ripe with his child. But not yet.

"Let's save that for another full moon. Let me have you to myself for a little while." Max lifted the hem of her shift and gently pulled it over her head. Her lush body was ripe, ready, and waiting for him. He could already smell the heady scent of her arousal.

He pressed a kiss to the glowing moon mark on her clavicle then gave it the gentlest of bites, fulfilling the requirement of marking her in front of his pack. Then he worked his way down her body with kisses and nips. Her nipples were already pebbled and begging for attention. He would spend plenty of time later seeing if he could make her come simply by sucking on them.

His mouth was watering for a different treat just then. Max dropped to his knees and grabbed Gal's thighs. She grabbed onto his shoulders and spread her legs for him. Any fear or anxiety she had about exposing herself in front of the rest of the pack was gone. There was only lust and love between them now.

She speared her hands into his hair and gave him a little tug. "Make me come, wolf."

"As you wish, my lady." Max dove in, licking and lashing and suckling at her clit. She groaned and pulled at his hair. He knew what her body needed and pushed two fingers into her hot, tight, wet cunt and pushed her body to give him the orgasm they both wanted. It didn't take long before she was moaning his name.

She gasped, her body clenched, and she was lost to her first orgasm of the night. When her knees gave out under her, he was ready and grabbed her, pulling her down across his lap.

Gal rested her head against his chest for a minute

breathing hard. "Man, you're good at that. Is it my turn. I've been having fantasies of sucking your cock under the stars."

"I thought I was the one with a dirty mouth?"

"Oh, ha ha. Please, proceed. I love when you talk dirty." She had the most adorable sloppy satisfied look on her face, and he couldn't resist kissing that dirty mouth.

"I promise you'll get plenty of opportunities to suck my cock to your heart's desire. But not tonight. I've been looking forward to this moment for too long and I can't wait any longer to take you, fuck you, make you mine again." Max slid Gal off his lap and helped her to get on her hands and knees.

Many wolves took their mates in the ritual as wolves. As his nod to that practice he wanted to fuck Gal from behind, his body covering hers. He slid his hand between her legs, pulling her juices from her cunt and across her thighs. Then he took his cock in his hand and set the very tip at her entrance.

"I'm so fucking hard just thinking about watching my cock slide in and out of your cunt, *kriska*."

"Do it, Max. I need you. Fill me, take me."

He loved that she was as hot for him as he was for her. He pushed all the way in, to his hilt and threw his head back. His wolf howled, laying claim to her, her body, her heart, her very soul.

His hips pistoned, and his cock glided in and out of her fast and hard. Her muscles squeezed tight around him, gripping him, giving them both an insane amount of pleasure. Max wanted to watch her pussy as he fucked it but he needed more of her and he bent over, pressing his chest to her back. He whispered into her ear. "I love you, Galyna."

"I love you so much, Max." She panted and her body quivered under him.

He wasn't going to last much longer and he needed to feel her come on his dick again. Max reached around and found her soft folds and hard nub. He pressed two fingers against it and pounded into her pussy, letting his fingers stroke her to match his rhythm.

"Max, yes, Max. I'm going to come. Your cock feels so big. Ah, I'm coming. Yes, yes, Max." Galyna cried is name out into the night and her body went supernova around his.

Max's wolf rose up, claiming her body. His cock swelled and the knot at his base grew until he could only thrust once more into her and they were locked. His balls clenched and he yelled her name as he came, pumping everything he had into her body. The moon and the stars crashed down on him until there was only the light, him, and his love for Galyna.

He rolled them to the ground, laying his arm and leg out for her to rest on and together they rode the bliss of being together for a long time. When his cock released her, he slipped from her body and wrapped her into his arms.

"I love you. Galyna. My mate, my one true mate. I claim you, your love, and your soul as my own and give the same to you. Now and forever."

***

Get the the next book in the Alpha Wolves Want Curves book, Naughty Wolf here —> http://geni.us/NaughtyWolf

. . .

WOULD you like to read an extended epilogue for Galyna and Max?

Join my Curvy Connection and I'll send it to you right away!

Join here —> http://geni.us/MoreDirtyWolf

If you're already a member, check your email!

The Curvy Love Series

Curvy Diversion

Curvy Temptation

Curvy Persuasion

Curvy Domination (coming soon)

The Curvy Seduction Saga

Rebound

Rebellion

Reignite

Dragons Love Curves

Chase Me

Tease Me

Bite Me

Cage Me

Baby Me

Defy Me

ABOUT THE AUTHOR

Aidy Award is a curvy girl who kind of has a thing for stormtroopers. She's also the author of the popular Curvy Love series and the hot new Dragons Love Curves series. She writes curvy girl erotic romance, about real love, and dirty fun, with happy ever afters because every woman deserves great sex and even better romance, no matter her size, shape, or what the scale says.

Read the delicious tales of hot heroes and curvy heroines come to life under the covers and between the pages of Aidy's books. Then let her know because she really does want to hear from her readers.

Connect with Aidy on her website. www.AidyAward.com get her Curvy Connection, and join her Facebook Group - Aidy's Amazeballs.

41917926R00127

Printed in Poland
by Amazon Fulfillment
Poland Sp. z o.o., Wrocław